Disney

GRAPHIC NOVELS #1

PLANES

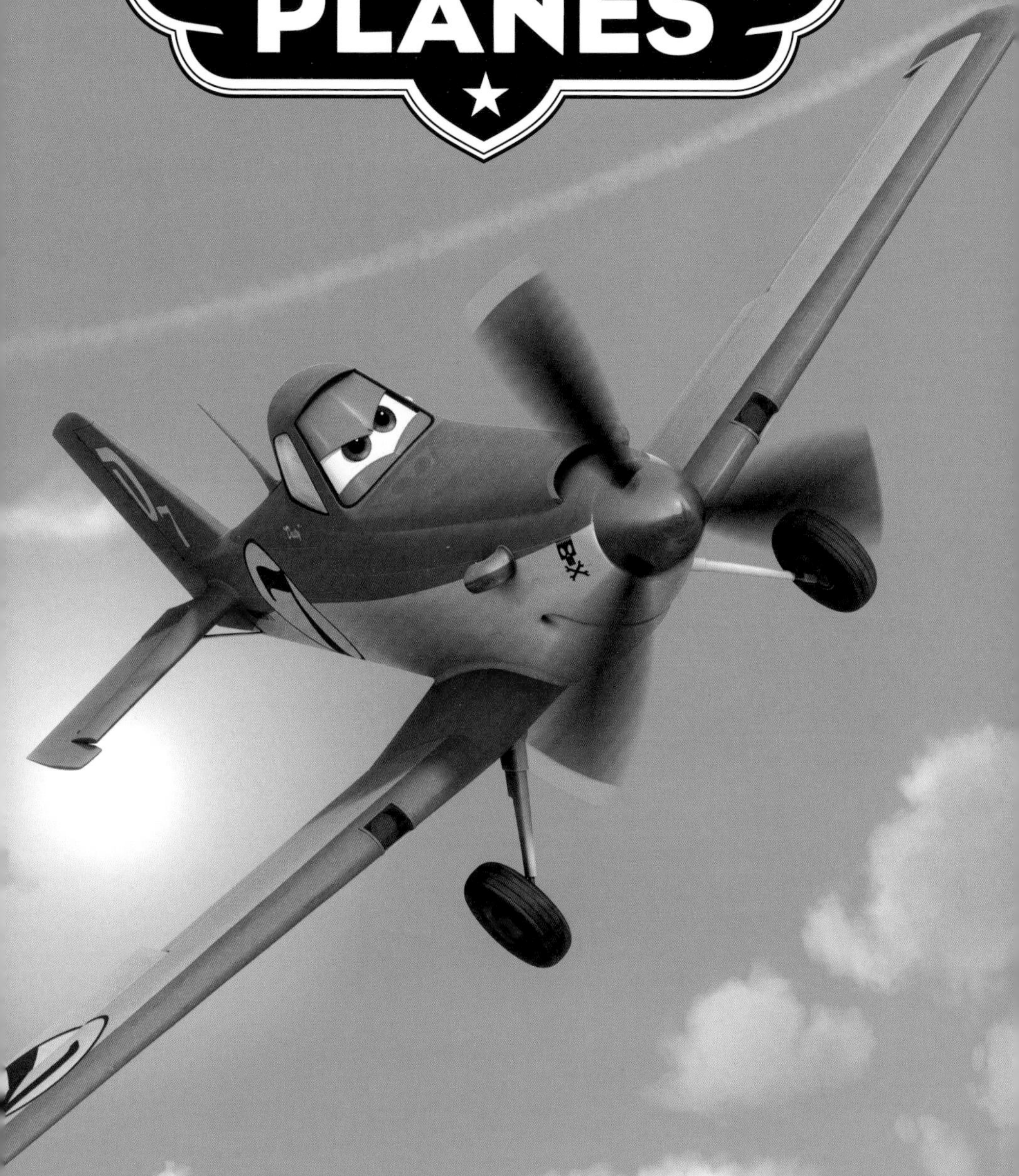

PAPERCUTZ

Disney Graphic Novels available from

PAPERCUTZ

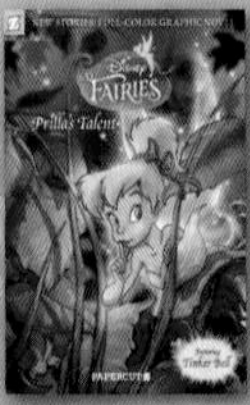

Graphic Novel #1
"Prilla's Talent"

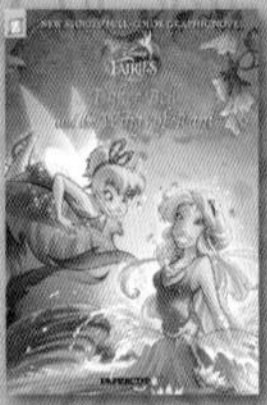

Graphic Novel #2
"Tinker Bell and the Wings of Rani"

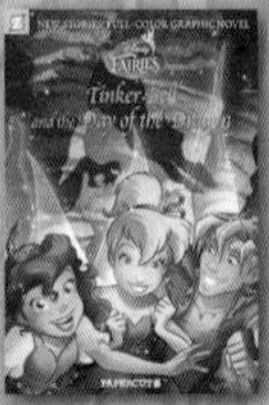

Graphic Novel #3
"Tinker Bell and the Day of the Dragon"

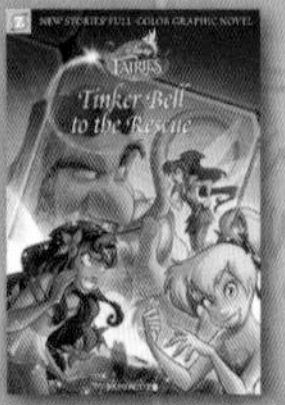

Graphic Novel #4
"Tinker Bell to the Rescue"

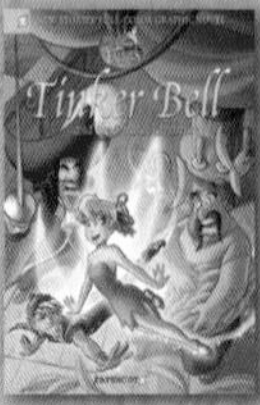

Graphic Novel #5
"Tinker Bell and the Pirate Adventure"

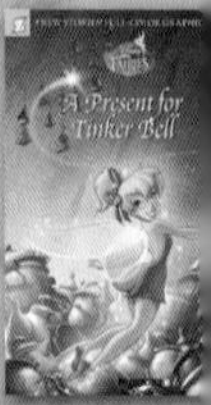

Graphic Nov
"A Present for Tinker B

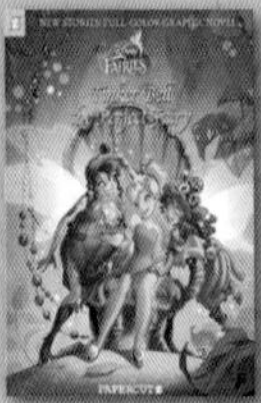

Graphic Novel #7
"Tinker Bell the Perfect Fairy"

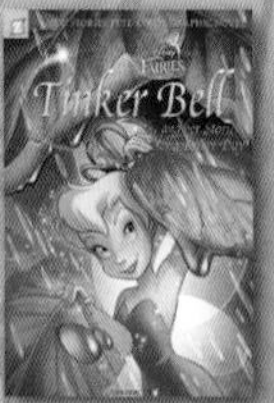

Graphic Novel #8
"Tinker Bell and her Stories for a Rainy Day"

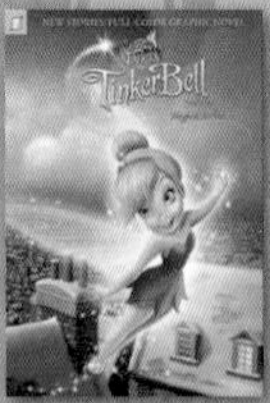

Graphic Novel #9
"Tinker Bell and her Magical Arrival"

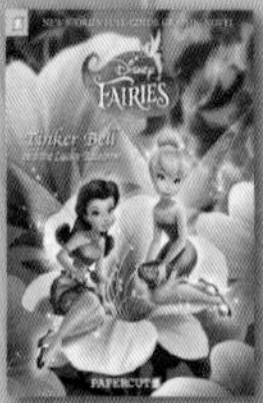

Graphic Novel #10
"Tinker Bell and the Lucky Rainbow"

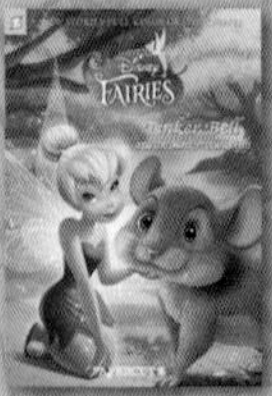

Graphic Novel #11
"Tinker Bell and the Most Precious Gift"

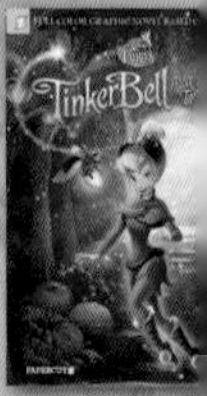

Graphic Nove
"Tinker Bell ar Lost Treasu

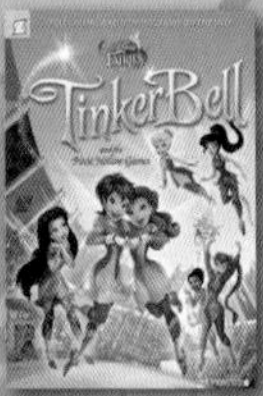

Graphic Novel #13
"Tinker Bell and the Pixie Hollow Games"

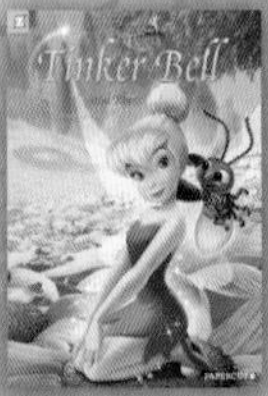

Graphic Novel #14
"Tinker Bell and Blaze"

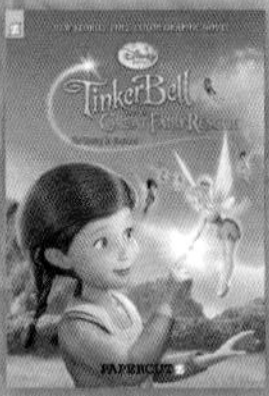

Tinker Bell and the Great Fairy Rescue

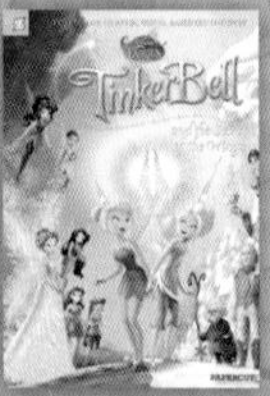

Graphic Novel #15
"Tinker Bell and the Secret of the Wings"

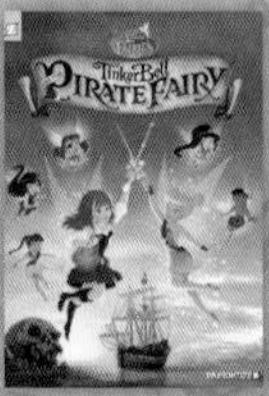

Graphic Novel #16
"Pirate Fairy"

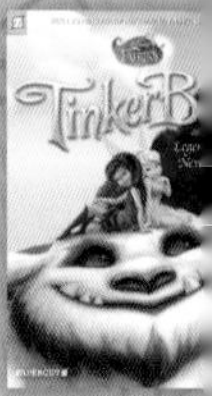

Graphic Nove
"Legend of NeverBeas

DISNEY FAIRIES graphic novels are available in paperback for $7.99 each; in hardcover for $12.99 each except #5, $6.99PB, $10.99HC. #6-15 are $7.99PB $11.99HC. Tinker Bell and the Great Fairy Rescue is $9.99 in hardcover only.
Available at booksellers everywhere.

See more at papercutz.com

Or you can order from us:
Please add $4.00 for postage and handling for first book, and add $1.00 for each additional book. Please make check payable to NBM Publishing.
Send to: Papercutz, 160 Broadway, Suite 700, East Wing, New York, NY 10038 or call 800 886 1223 (9-6 EST M-F) MC-Visa-Amex accepted.

COMING SOON

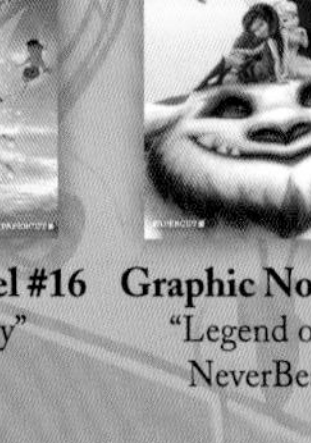

Graphic Novel #18
"Magical Friends"

Disney
GRAPHIC NOVELS #1

PLANES

"Livin' the Dream"

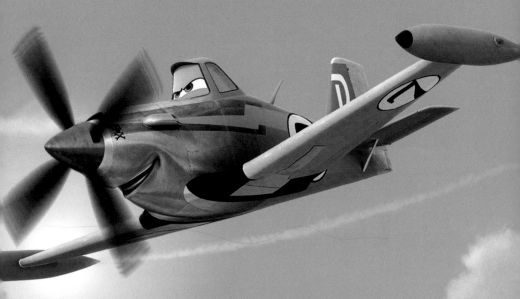

PAPERCUTZ
New York

Disney
GRAPHIC NOVELS #1

PLANES

"Livin' the Dream"

Manuscript Adaptation – Alessandro Sisti

(Based on the story by John Lasseter, Klay Hall, and Jeffrey M. Howard
and the screenplay by Jeffrey M. Howard.)

Layout – Roberto Di Salvo, Grafimated, Lucio Leoni
Pencil – Lucio Leoni, Gianfranco Florio, Paco Desiato
Paint – Massimo Rocca, Paco Desiato
Artist Coordination – Tomatofarm
Editorial Pages – Co-d S.r.l. – Milano, Dario Cassani
Pre-Press – Lito Milano S.r.l.
Special Thanks to: Klay Hall, Paul Gerard, Heather Knowles, Jean-Paul Orpinas

DISNEY PUBLISHING WORLDWIDE
Global Magazines, Comics and Partworks

Vice President, Global Magazines and New IP: Gianfranco Cordara
Editorial Director: Guido Frazzini
Editorial Team: Antonella Donola, Virpi Korhonen
Design: Enrico Soave
Art: Caroline LaVelle Egan, Charles E. Pickens
Project Management: Dorothea DePrisco (Director), Mariantonietta Galla, Camilla Vedove
Portfolio Management: Olivia Ciancarelli (Director), Josefina Pierucci

Production – Dawn K. Guzzo
Production Coordinator – Jeff Whitman
Associate Editor – Bethany Bryan
Jim Salicrup
Editor-in-Chief

ISBN: 978-1-62991-286-8 paperback edition
ISBN: 978-1-62991-287-5 hardcover edition

Printed in Canada
August 2015 by Friesens Printing
1 Printer Way
Altona, MB R0G 0B0

Papercutz books may be purchased for business or promotional use.
For information on bulk purchases please contact Macmillan Corporate
and Premium Sales Department at (800) 221-7945 x5442.

Distributed by Macmillan
First Papercutz Printing

FSC
www.fsc.org
MIX
Paper from
responsible sources
FSC® C006398

Disney
GRAPHIC NOVELS #1

PLANES

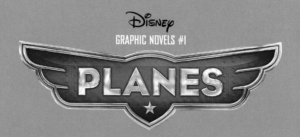

CONTENTS

PROPWASH JUNCTION

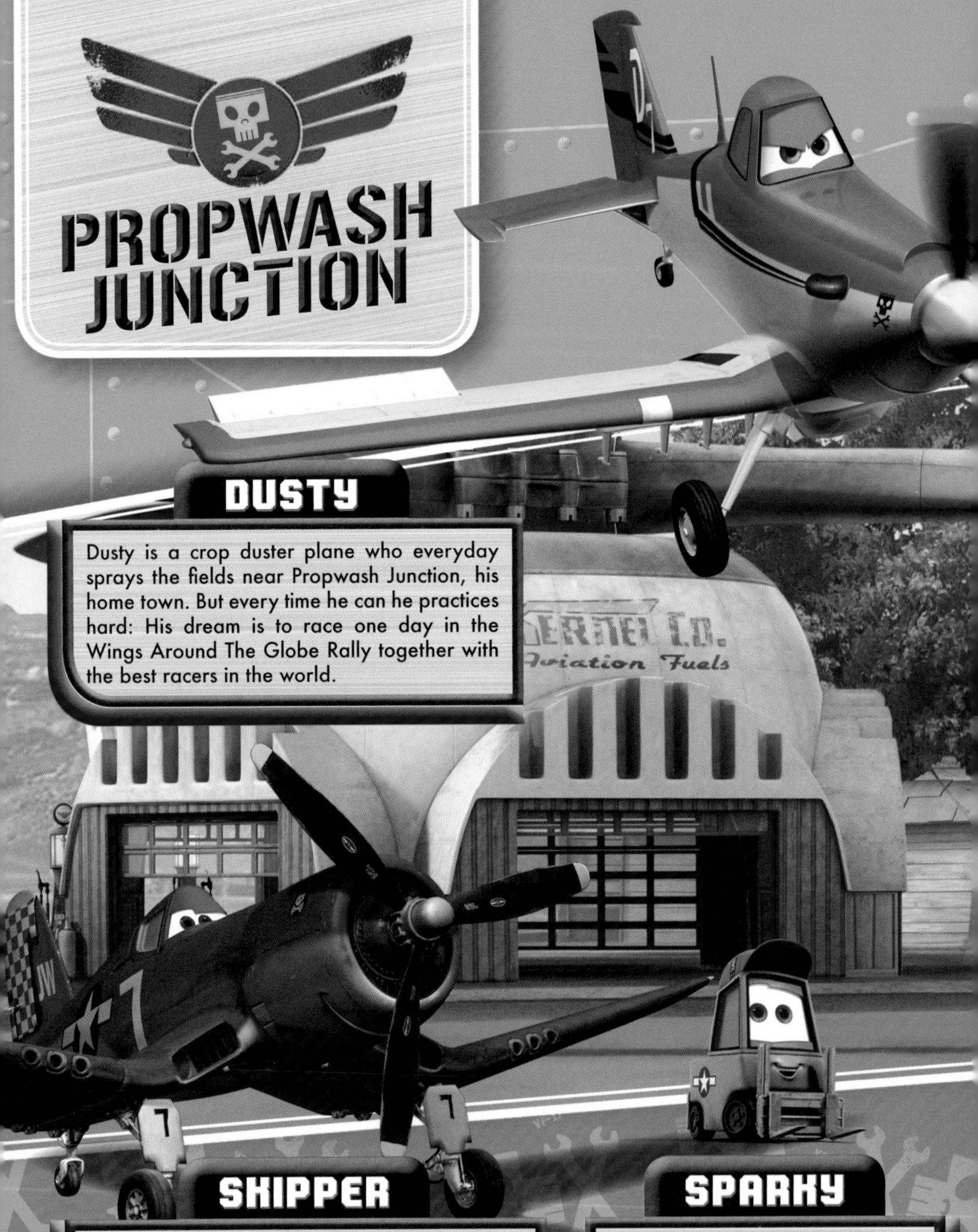
Aviation Fuels

DUSTY

Dusty is a crop duster plane who everyday sprays the fields near Propwash Junction, his home town. But every time he can he practices hard: His dream is to race one day in the Wings Around The Globe Rally together with the best racers in the world.

SKIPPER

Skipper Riley is the old navy plane who teaches Dusty the techniques to fly a little higher. Came to Propwash Junction after the war, he lives a quiet life in town, but this ex top instructor has a secret in his past navy career and Dusty will discover it.

SPARKY

This cheerful and trusty friend of Skipper's has been by his side for many years and he pushes him wherever he needs to go. Sparky is always ready to help in whatever job needs to be done in the hangar.

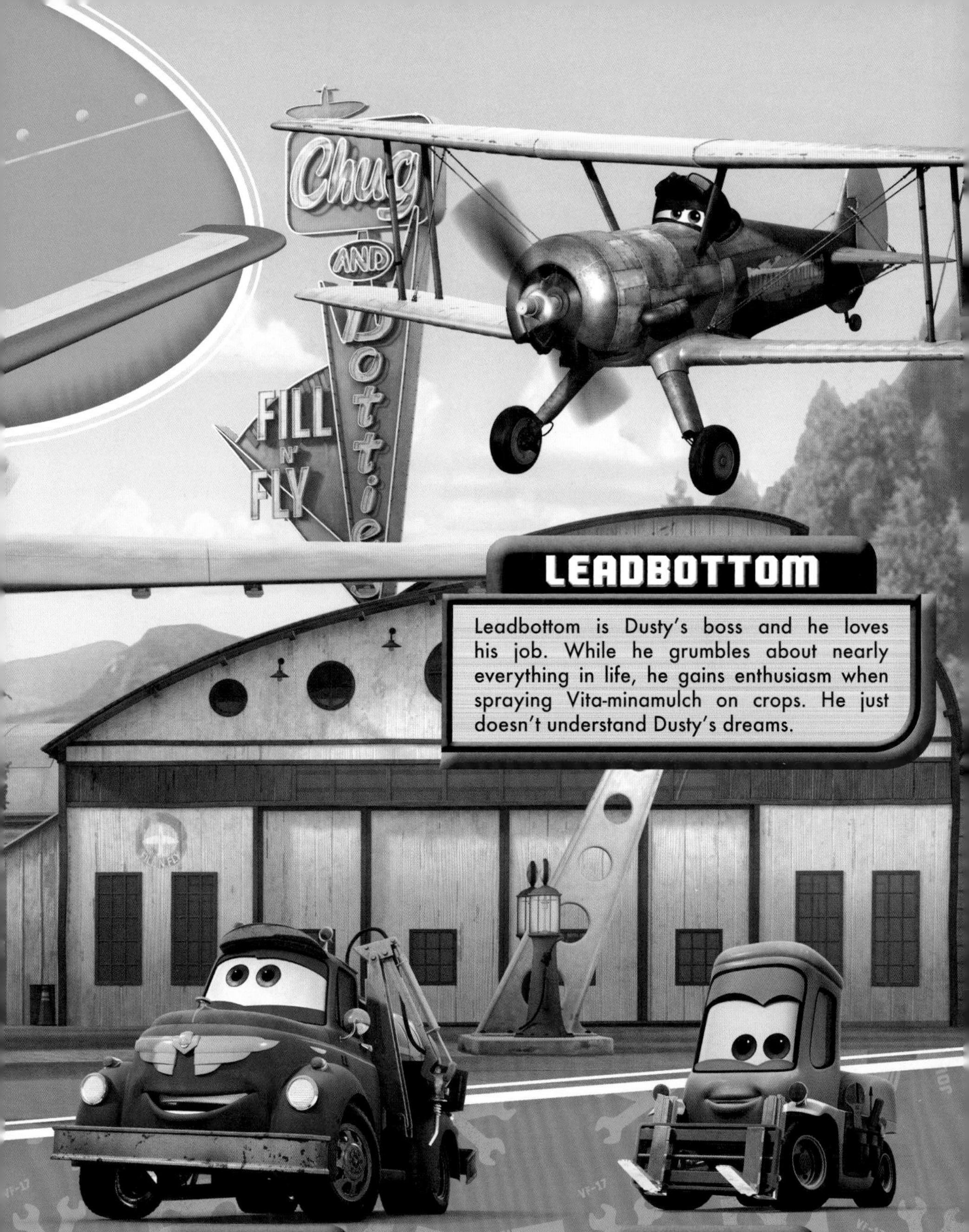
Chug
AND
Dottie
FILL
N'
FLY

LEADBOTTOM

Leadbottom is Dusty's boss and he loves his job. While he grumbles about nearly everything in life, he gains enthusiasm when spraying Vita-minamulch on crops. He just doesn't understand Dusty's dreams.

CHUG

Chug is Dusty's best friend and his only supporter in his dream to become a racer. Since Chug has never really travelled outside of Propwash Junction, he's even more engaged in Dusty's journey around the world.

DOTTIE

Together with Chug, this forklift tug runs the Fill 'n' Fly service station. Dottie loves confusing people by using technical language. She's Dusty's mechanic and she knows the limits of his engine; that's why she's a bit worried about his racing.

THE RACERS

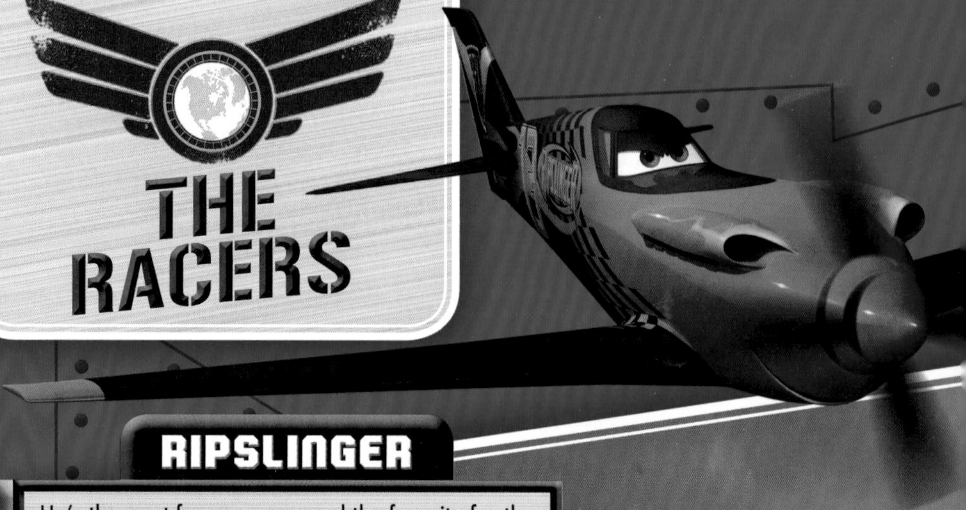

RIPSLINGER

He's the most famous racer and the favorite for the upcoming Wings Around The Globe Rally. In the beginning, Rip is Dusty's racing idol, but when the crop duster has the chance to meet him, he sees how arrogant and mean spirited Rip is.

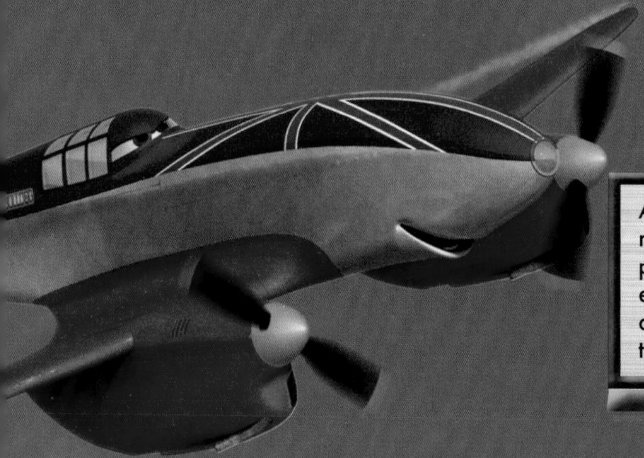

BULLDOG

As the oldest racer of all, he often remembers when GPS wasn't used and planes navigated by stars. He disregards electronic devices and values fairness above all. He has been racing more than the others and he's still among the top.

ROCHELLE

She's the French Canadian champion and has a talent for fast travel. Rochelle is the target of El Chupacabra's constant romantic attentions but she seems to be more focused on winning.

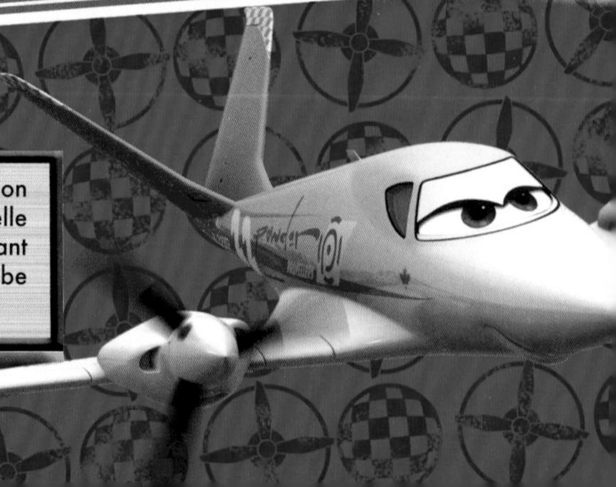

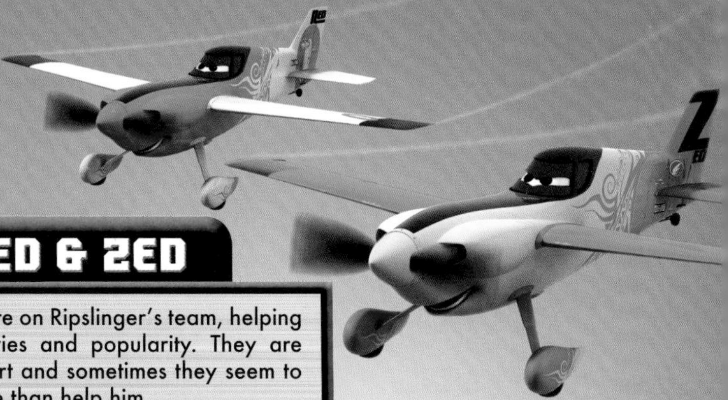

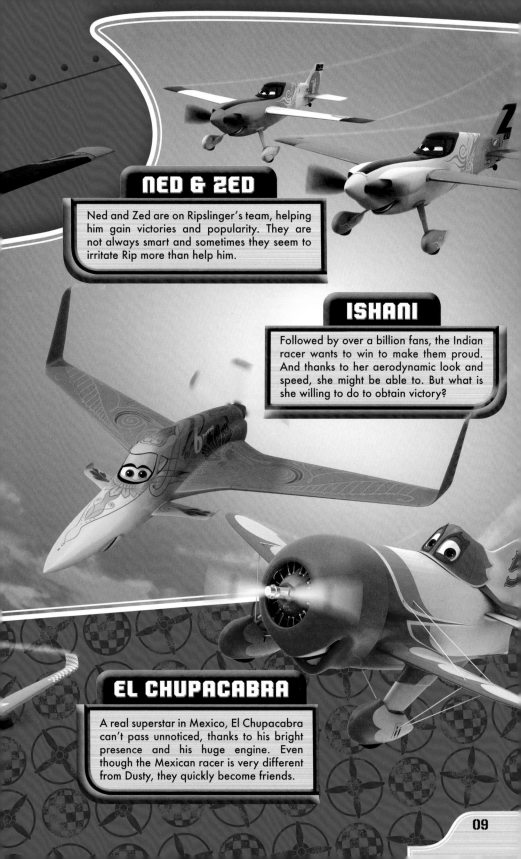

NED & ZED

Ned and Zed are on Ripslinger's team, helping him gain victories and popularity. They are not always smart and sometimes they seem to irritate Rip more than help him.

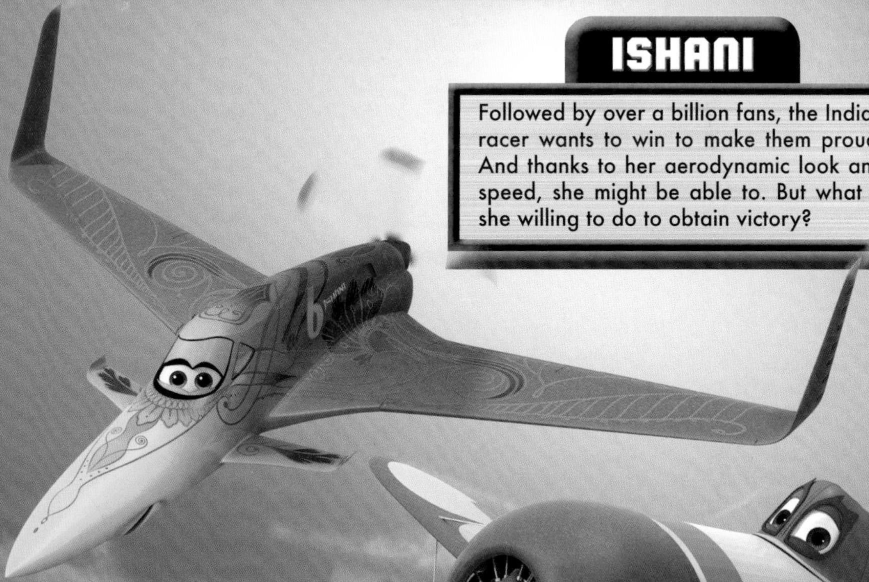

ISHANI

Followed by over a billion fans, the Indian racer wants to win to make them proud. And thanks to her aerodynamic look and speed, she might be able to. But what is she willing to do to obtain victory?

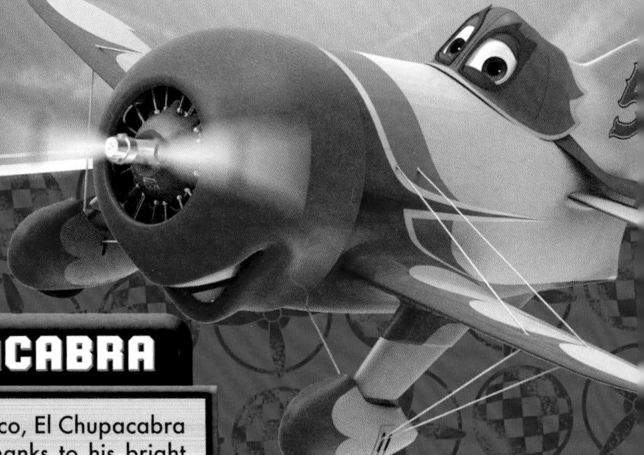

EL CHUPACABRA

A real superstar in Mexico, El Chupacabra can't pass unnoticed, thanks to his bright presence and his huge engine. Even though the Mexican racer is very different from Dusty, they quickly become friends.

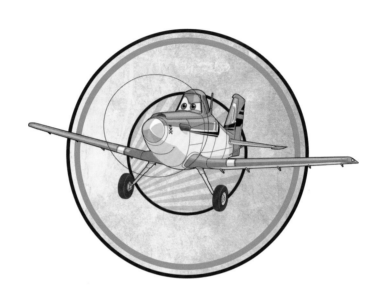

"LIVIN' THE DREAM"
DUSTY CROPHOPPER

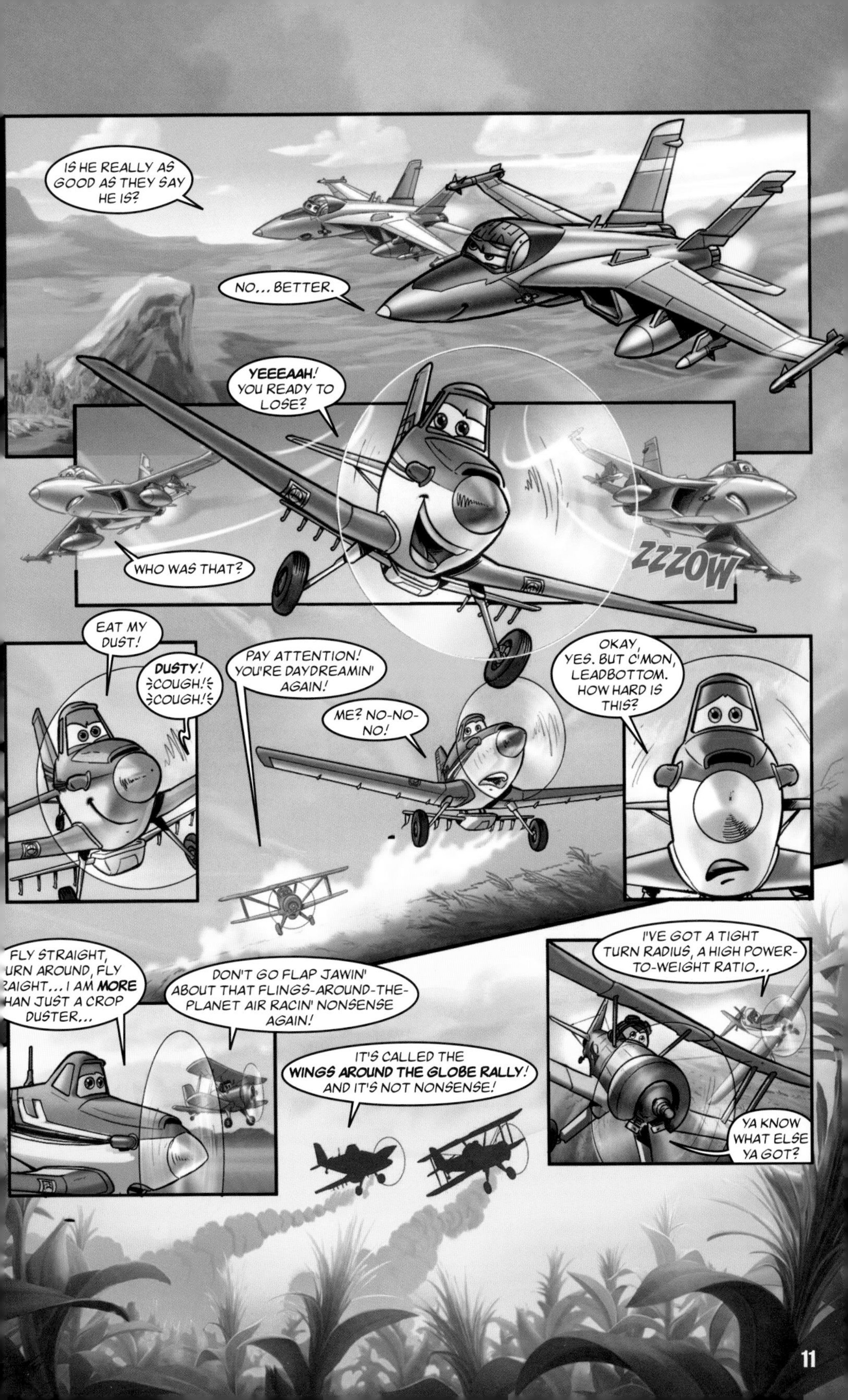

IS HE REALLY AS GOOD AS THEY SAY HE IS?
NO... BETTER.
YEEEAAH! YOU READY TO LOSE?
WHO WAS THAT?
ZZZOW
EAT MY DUST!
DUSTY! COUGH! COUGH!
PAY ATTENTION! YOU'RE DAYDREAMIN' AGAIN!
ME? NO-NO-NO!
OKAY, YES. BUT C'MON, LEADBOTTOM. HOW HARD IS THIS?
FLY STRAIGHT, URN AROUND, FLY RAIGHT... I AM MORE HAN JUST A CROP DUSTER...
DON'T GO FLAP JAWIN' ABOUT THAT FLINGS-AROUND-THE-PLANET AIR RACIN' NONSENSE AGAIN!
IT'S CALLED THE WINGS AROUND THE GLOBE RALLY! AND IT'S NOT NONSENSE!
I'VE GOT A TIGHT TURN RADIUS, A HIGH POWER-TO-WEIGHT RATIO...
YA KNOW WHAT ELSE YA GOT?

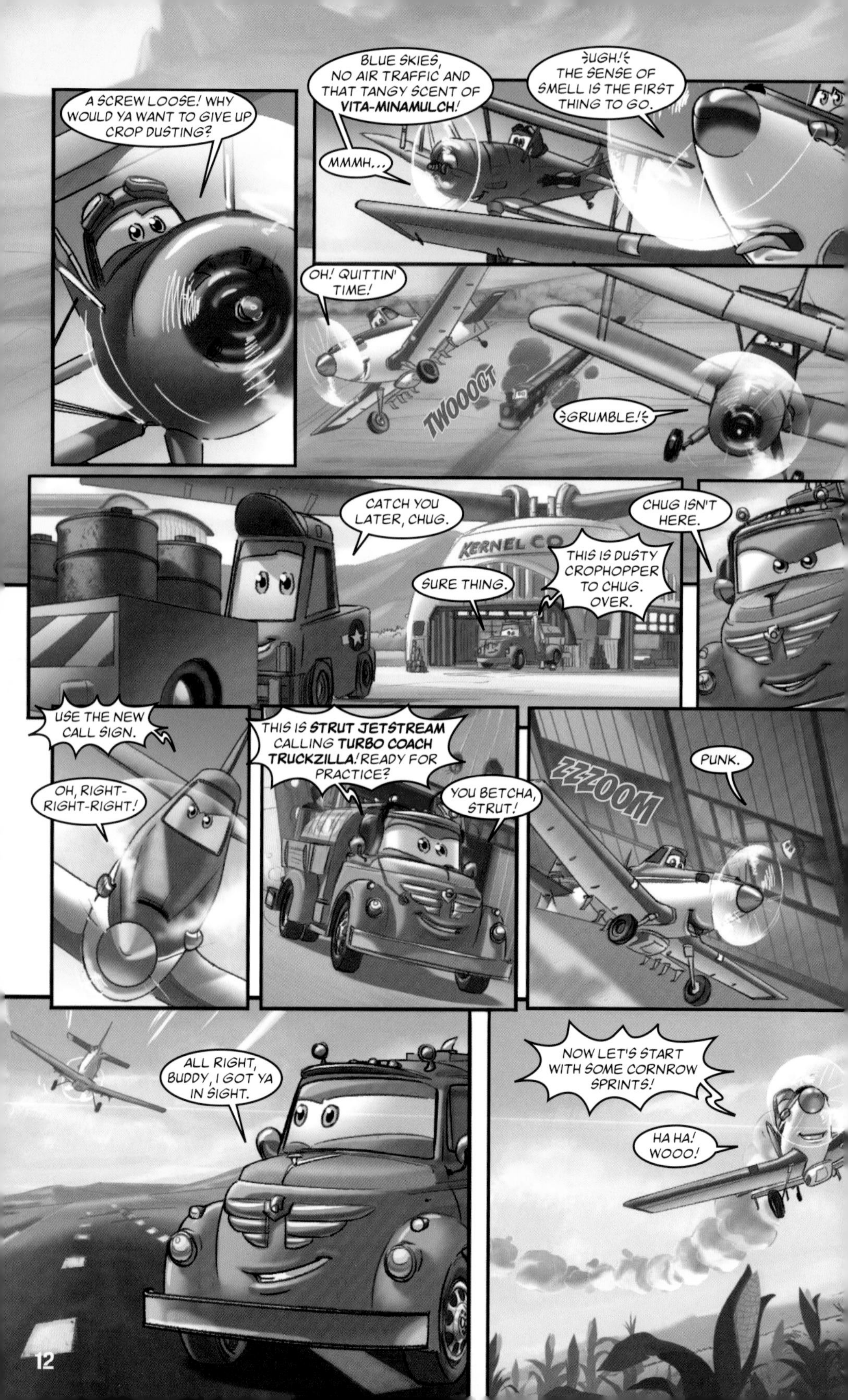

A SCREW LOOSE! WHY WOULD YA WANT TO GIVE UP CROP DUSTING?
BLUE SKIES, NO AIR TRAFFIC AND THAT TANGY SCENT OF VITA-MINAMULCH!
MMMH...
UGH! THE SENSE OF SMELL IS THE FIRST THING TO GO.
OH! QUITTIN' TIME!
TWOOOOT
GRUMBLE!
CATCH YOU LATER, CHUG.
KERNEL CO
SURE THING.
THIS IS DUSTY CROPHOPPER TO CHUG. OVER.
CHUG ISN'T HERE.
USE THE NEW CALL SIGN.
OH, RIGHT-RIGHT-RIGHT!
THIS IS STRUT JETSTREAM CALLING TURBO COACH TRUCKZILLA! READY FOR PRACTICE?
YOU BETCHA, STRUT!
ZZZOOM
PUNK.
ALL RIGHT, BUDDY, I GOT YA IN SIGHT.
NOW LET'S START WITH SOME CORNROW SPRINTS!
HA HA! WOOO!

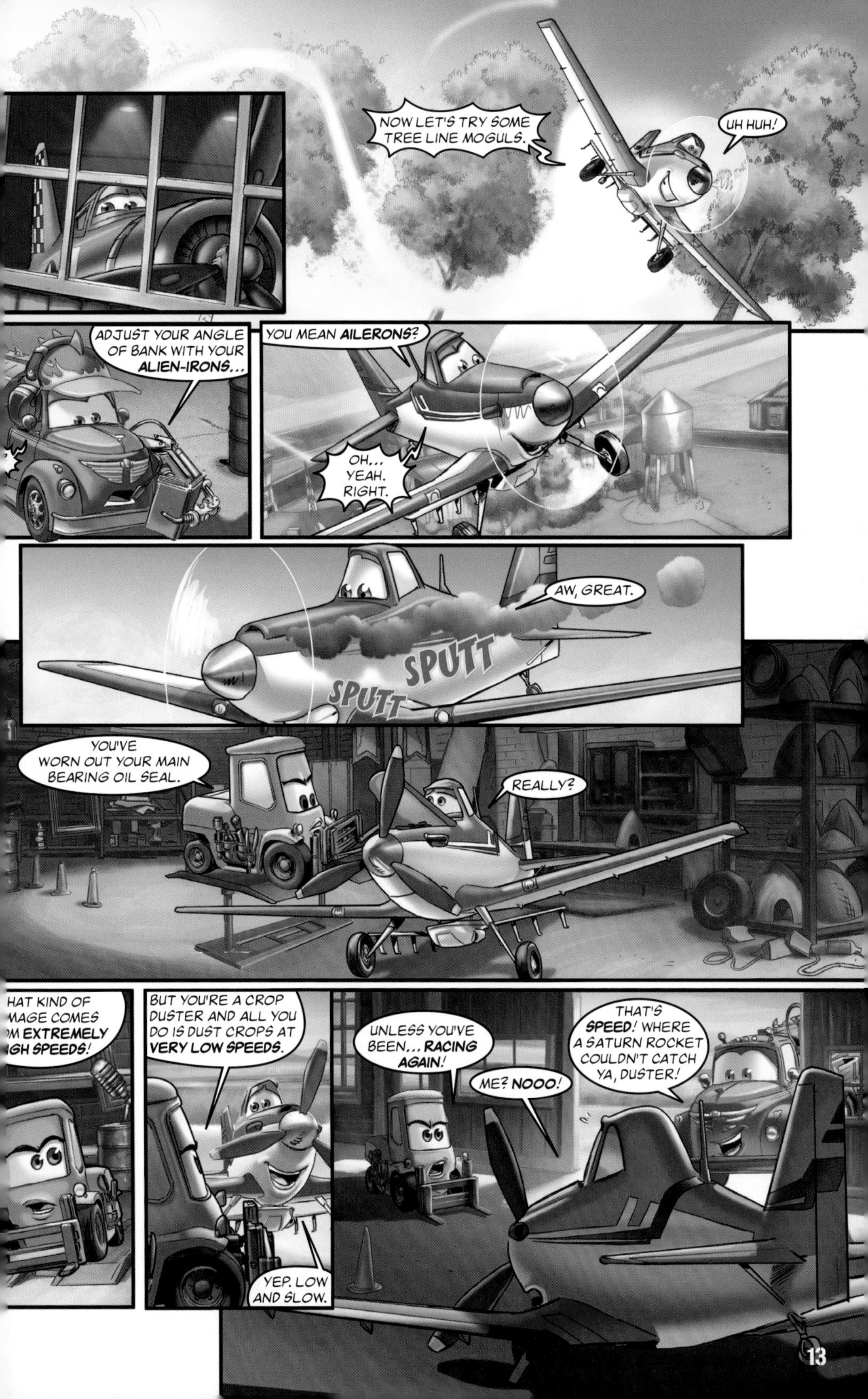
NOW LET'S TRY SOME TREE LINE MOGULS.
UH HUH!
ADJUST YOUR ANGLE OF BANK WITH YOUR **ALIEN-IRONS...**
YOU MEAN **AILERONS?**
OH... YEAH. RIGHT.
AW, GREAT.
SPUTT
SPUTT
YOU'VE WORN OUT YOUR MAIN BEARING OIL SEAL.
REALLY?
HAT KIND OF MAGE COMES M **EXTREMELY GH SPEEDS!**
BUT YOU'RE A CROP DUSTER AND ALL YOU DO IS DUST CROPS AT **VERY LOW SPEEDS.**
YEP. LOW AND SLOW.
UNLESS YOU'VE BEEN... **RACING AGAIN!**
ME? **NOOO!**
THAT'S **SPEED!** WHERE A SATURN ROCKET COULDN'T CATCH YA, DUSTER!

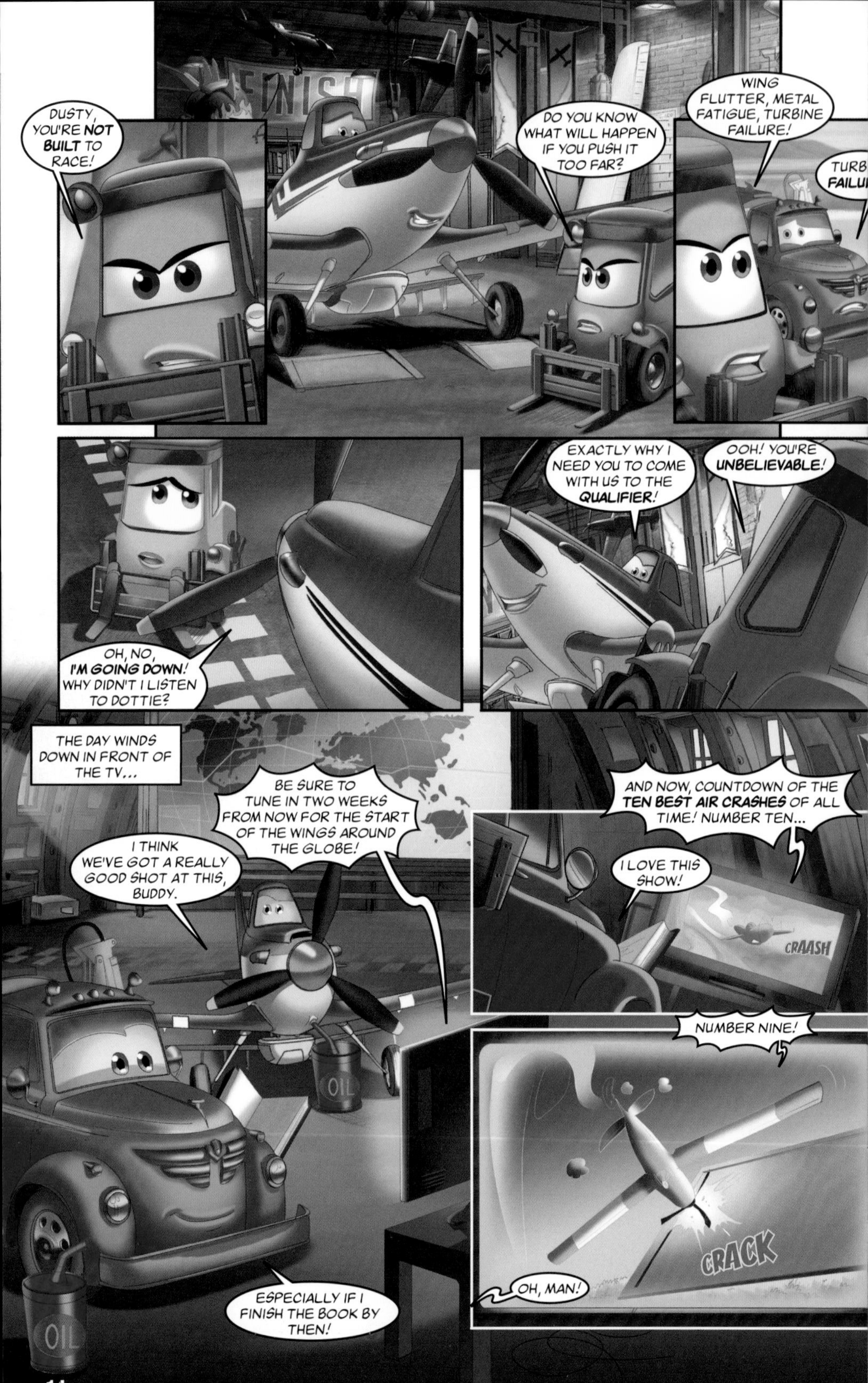
DUSTY, YOU'RE **NOT BUILT** TO RACE!
DO YOU KNOW WHAT WILL HAPPEN IF YOU PUSH IT TOO FAR?
WING FLUTTER, METAL FATIGUE, TURBINE FAILURE!
OH, NO, **I'M GOING DOWN**! WHY DIDN'T I LISTEN TO DOTTIE?
EXACTLY WHY I NEED YOU TO COME WITH US TO THE **QUALIFIER**!
OOH! YOU'RE **UNBELIEVABLE**!
THE DAY WINDS DOWN IN FRONT OF THE TV...
BE SURE TO TUNE IN TWO WEEKS FROM NOW FOR THE START OF THE WINGS AROUND THE GLOBE!
I THINK WE'VE GOT A REALLY GOOD SHOT AT THIS, BUDDY.
ESPECIALLY IF I FINISH THE BOOK BY THEN!
AND NOW, COUNTDOWN OF THE **TEN BEST AIR CRASHES** OF ALL TIME! NUMBER TEN...
I LOVE THIS SHOW!
CRAASH
NUMBER NINE!
CRACK
OH, MAN!

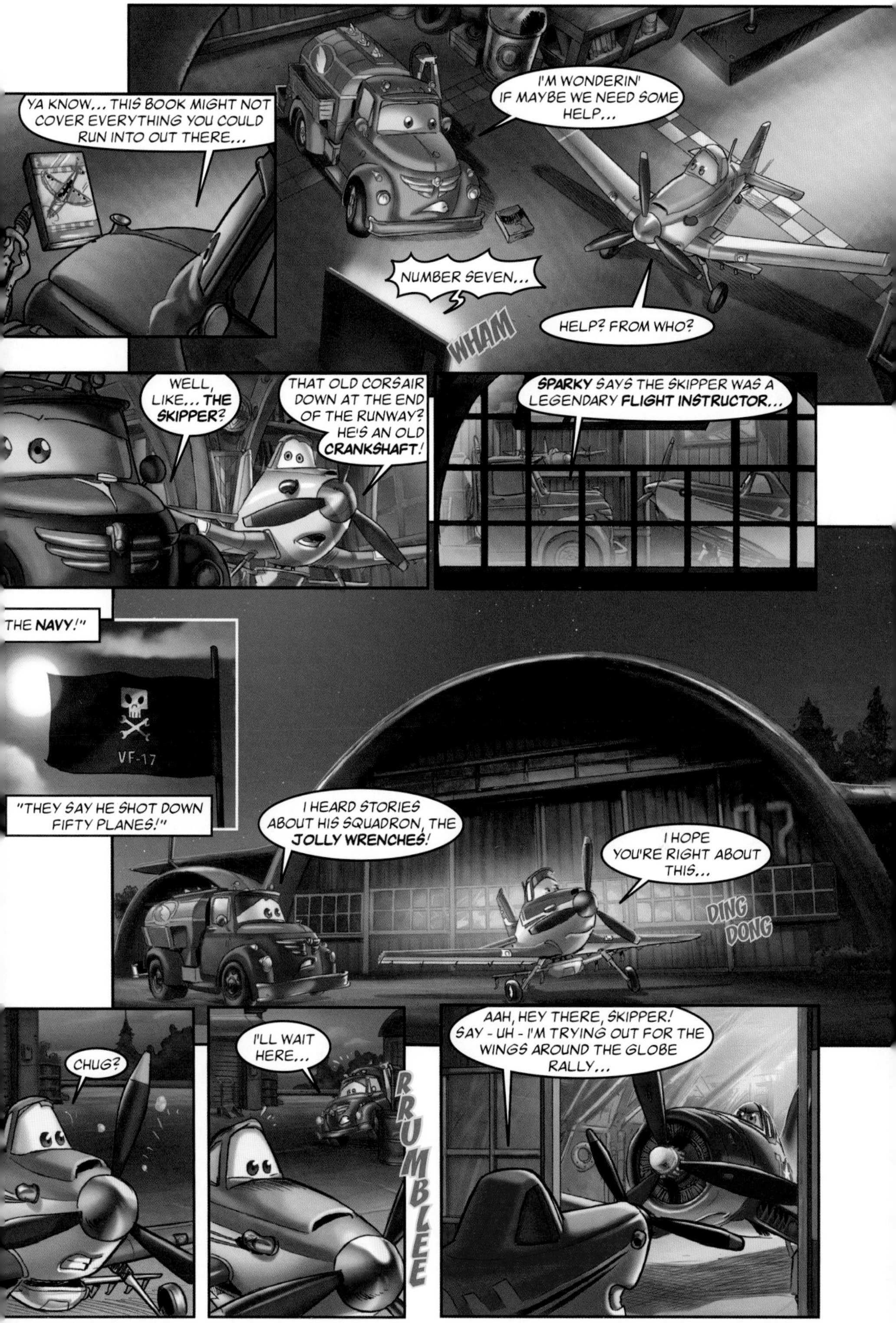
YA KNOW... THIS BOOK MIGHT NOT COVER EVERYTHING YOU COULD RUN INTO OUT THERE...
I'M WONDERIN' IF MAYBE WE NEED SOME HELP...
NUMBER SEVEN...
WHAM
HELP? FROM WHO?
WELL, LIKE... THE SKIPPER?
THAT OLD CORSAIR DOWN AT THE END OF THE RUNWAY? HE'S AN OLD CRANKSHAFT!
SPARKY SAYS THE SKIPPER WAS A LEGENDARY FLIGHT INSTRUCTOR...
THE NAVY!"
VF-17
"THEY SAY HE SHOT DOWN FIFTY PLANES!"
I HEARD STORIES ABOUT HIS SQUADRON, THE JOLLY WRENCHES!
I HOPE YOU'RE RIGHT ABOUT THIS...
DING DONG
CHUG?
I'LL WAIT HERE...
RRUMBLEE
AAH, HEY THERE, SKIPPER! SAY - UH - I'M TRYING OUT FOR THE WINGS AROUND THE GLOBE RALLY...

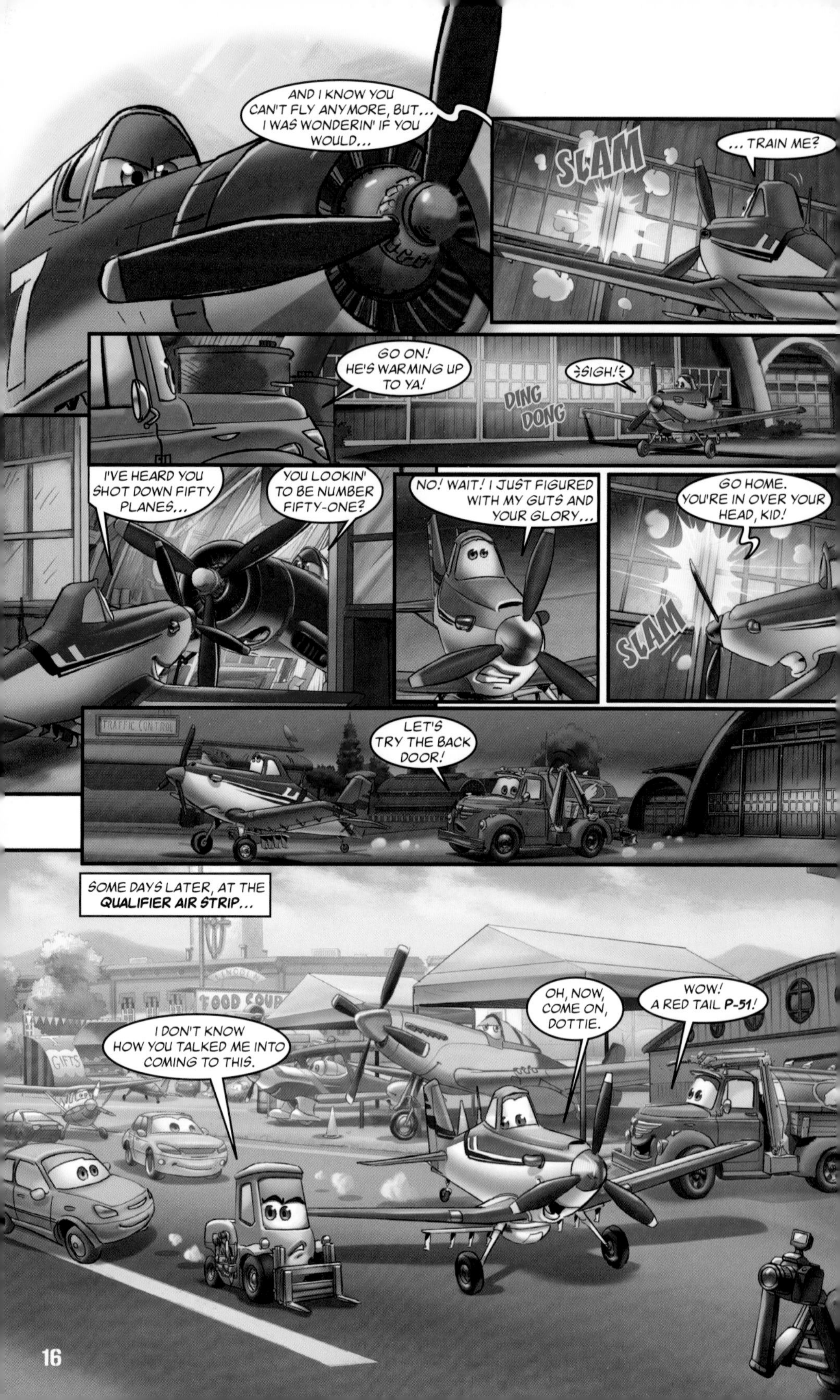
AND I KNOW YOU CAN'T FLY ANYMORE, BUT... I WAS WONDERIN' IF YOU WOULD...
SLAM
...TRAIN ME?
GO ON! HE'S WARMING UP TO YA!
SIGH!
DING DONG
I'VE HEARD YOU SHOT DOWN FIFTY PLANES...
YOU LOOKIN' TO BE NUMBER FIFTY-ONE?
NO! WAIT! I JUST FIGURED WITH MY GUTS AND YOUR GLORY...
GO HOME. YOU'RE IN OVER YOUR HEAD, KID!
SLAM
TRAFFIC CONTROL
LET'S TRY THE BACK DOOR!
SOME DAYS LATER, AT THE QUALIFIER AIR STRIP...
FOOD COUR
GIFTS
I DON'T KNOW HOW YOU TALKED ME INTO COMING TO THIS.
OH, NOW, COME ON, DOTTIE.
WOW! A RED TAIL P-51!

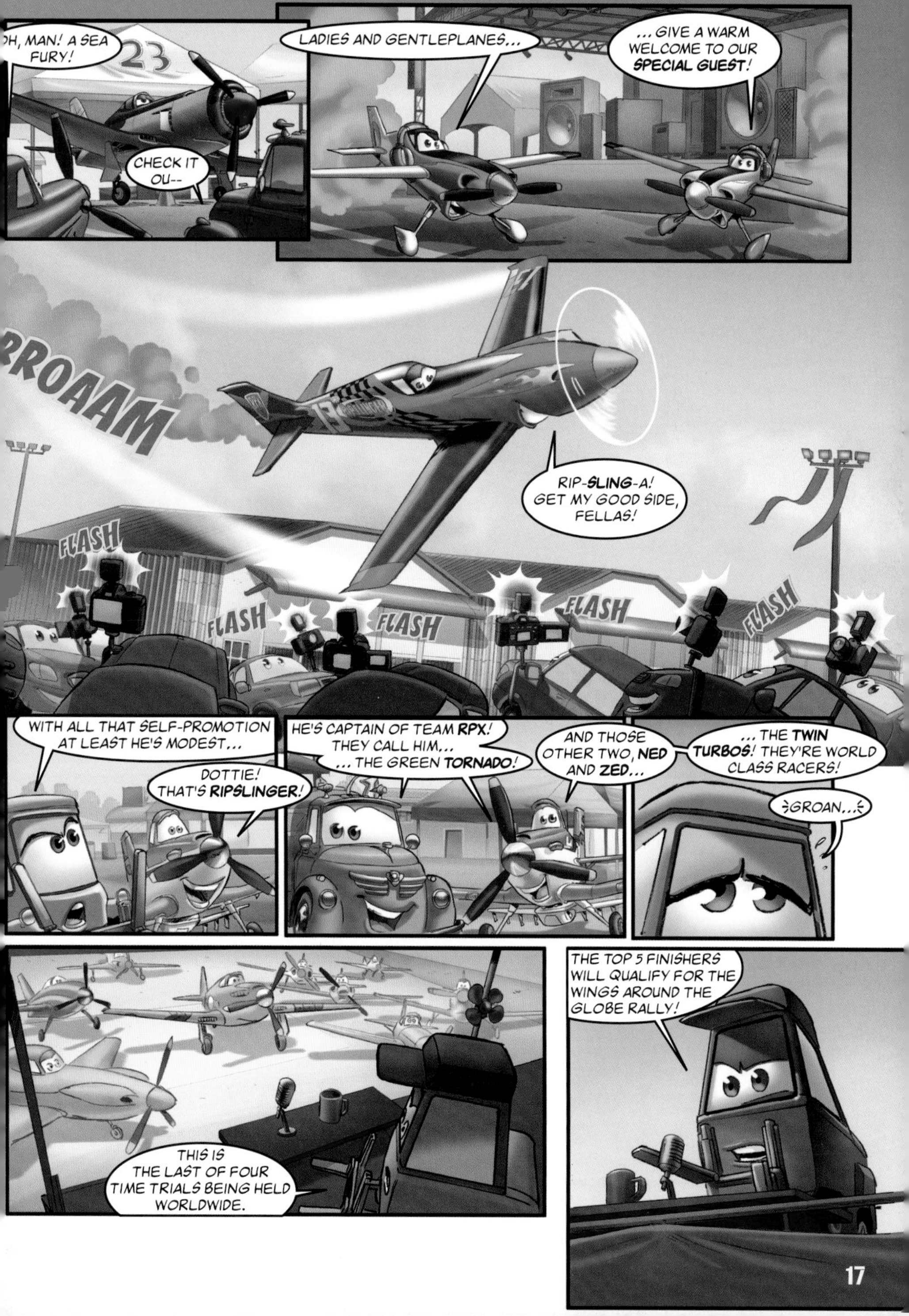

...H, MAN! A SEA FURY!
CHECK IT OU--
LADIES AND GENTLEPLANES...
... GIVE A WARM WELCOME TO OUR SPECIAL GUEST!
RROAAAM
RIP-SLING-A! GET MY GOOD SIDE, FELLAS!
FLASH
FLASH
FLASH
FLASH
FLASH
WITH ALL THAT SELF-PROMOTION AT LEAST HE'S MODEST...
DOTTIE! THAT'S RIPSLINGER!
HE'S CAPTAIN OF TEAM RPX! THEY CALL HIM...
... THE GREEN TORNADO!
AND THOSE OTHER TWO, NED AND ZED...
... THE TWIN TURBOS! THEY'RE WORLD CLASS RACERS!
GROAN...
THIS IS THE LAST OF FOUR TIME TRIALS BEING HELD WORLDWIDE.
THE TOP 5 FINISHERS WILL QUALIFY FOR THE WINGS AROUND THE GLOBE RALLY!

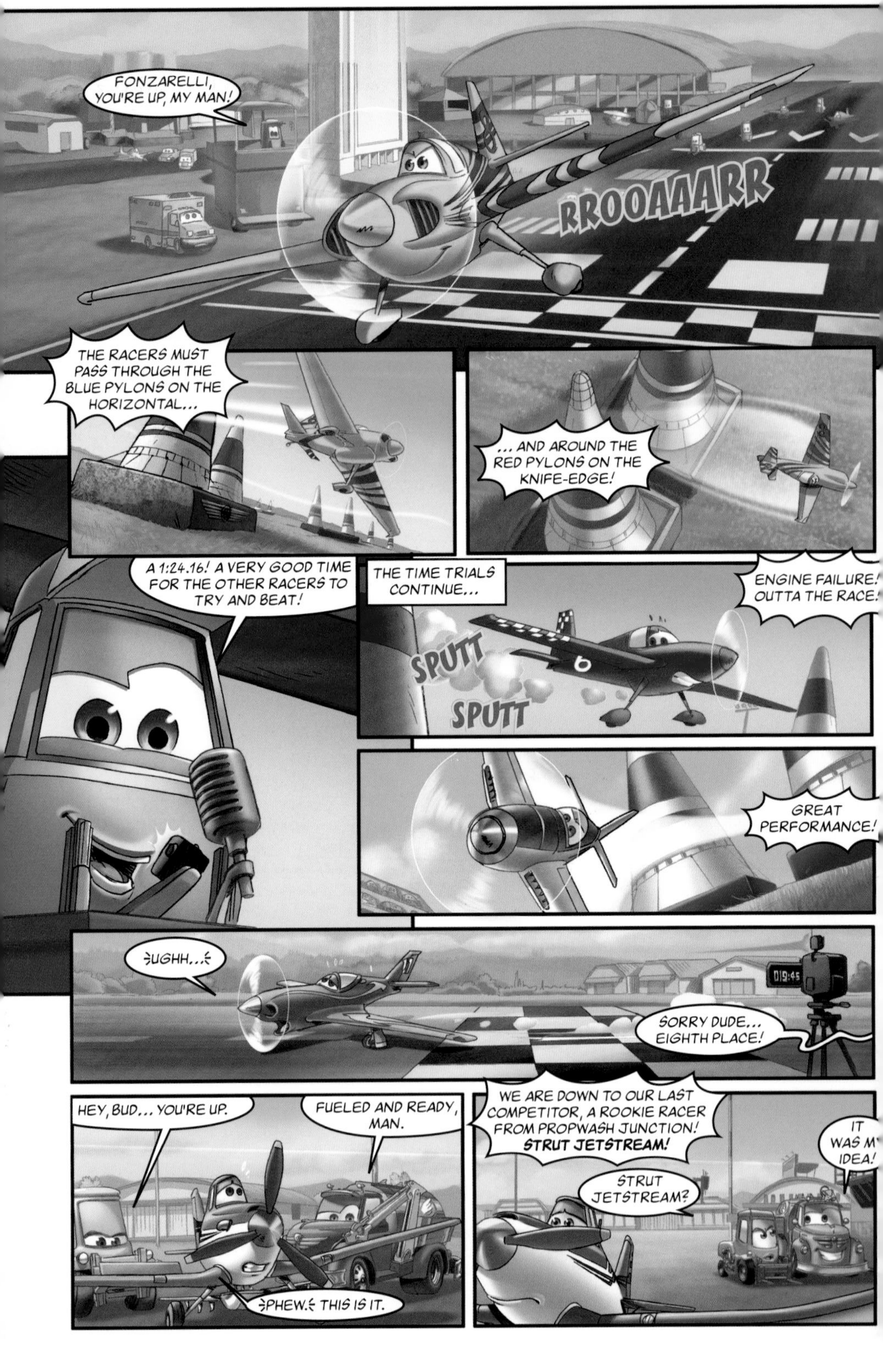
FONZARELLI, YOU'RE UP, MY MAN!
RROOAAARR
THE RACERS MUST PASS THROUGH THE BLUE PYLONS ON THE HORIZONTAL...
... AND AROUND THE RED PYLONS ON THE KNIFE-EDGE!
A 1:24.16! A VERY GOOD TIME FOR THE OTHER RACERS TO TRY AND BEAT!
THE TIME TRIALS CONTINUE...
ENGINE FAILURE! OUTTA THE RACE!
SPUTT
SPUTT
GREAT PERFORMANCE!
UGHH...
SORRY DUDE... EIGHTH PLACE!
HEY, BUD... YOU'RE UP.
FUELED AND READY, MAN.
PHEW. THIS IS IT.
WE ARE DOWN TO OUR LAST COMPETITOR, A ROOKIE RACER FROM PROPWASH JUNCTION! **STRUT JETSTREAM!**
STRUT JETSTREAM?
IT WAS M IDEA!

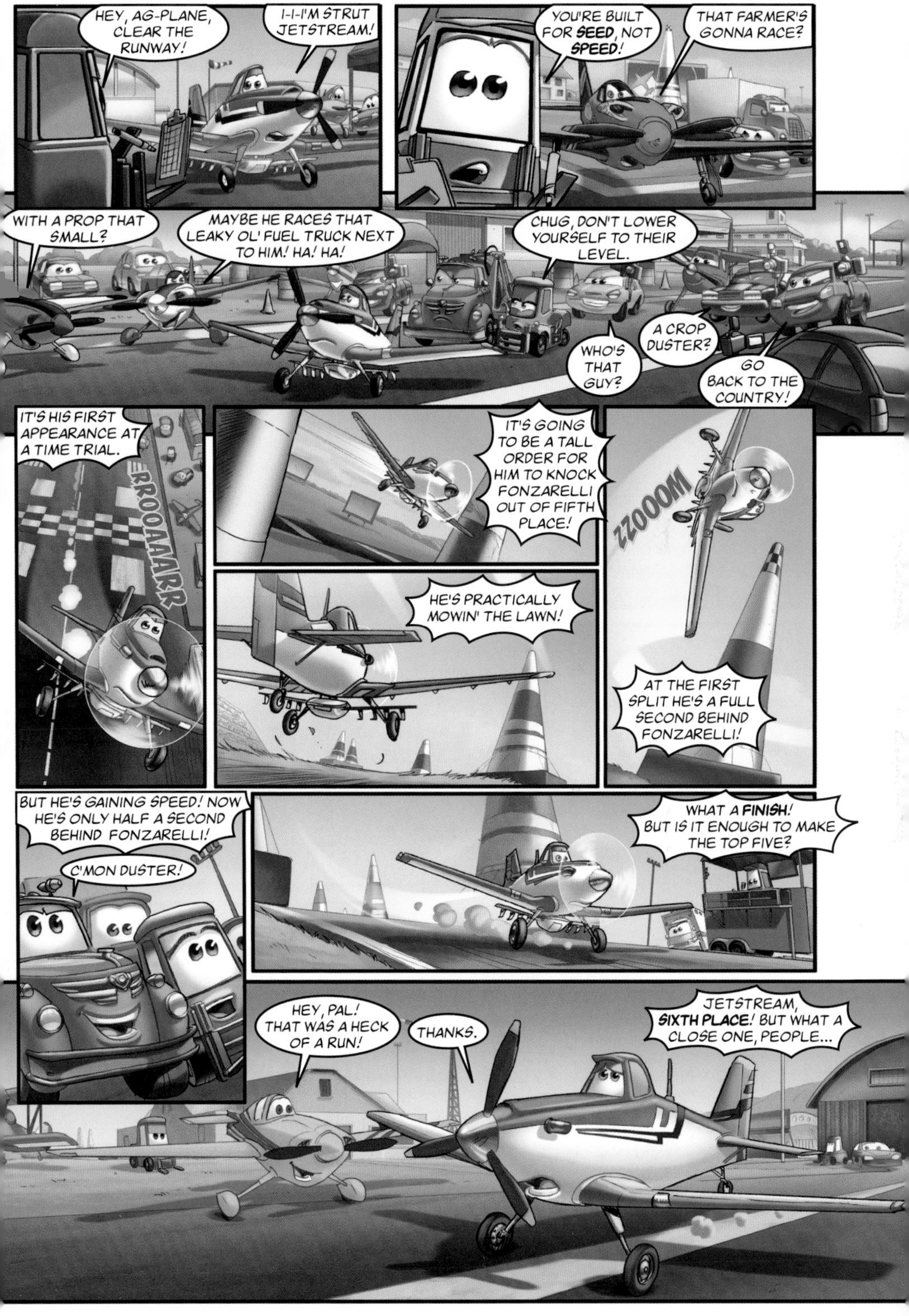
HEY, AG-PLANE, CLEAR THE RUNWAY!
I-I-I'M STRUT JETSTREAM!
YOU'RE BUILT FOR SEED, NOT SPEED!
THAT FARMER'S GONNA RACE?
WITH A PROP THAT SMALL?
MAYBE HE RACES THAT LEAKY OL' FUEL TRUCK NEXT TO HIM! HA! HA!
CHUG, DON'T LOWER YOURSELF TO THEIR LEVEL.
WHO'S THAT GUY?
A CROP DUSTER?
GO BACK TO THE COUNTRY!
IT'S HIS FIRST APPEARANCE AT A TIME TRIAL.
RROOAAARR
IT'S GOING TO BE A TALL ORDER FOR HIM TO KNOCK FONZARELLI OUT OF FIFTH PLACE!
ZZOOOM
HE'S PRACTICALLY MOWIN' THE LAWN!
AT THE FIRST SPLIT HE'S A FULL SECOND BEHIND FONZARELLI!
BUT HE'S GAINING SPEED! NOW HE'S ONLY HALF A SECOND BEHIND FONZARELLI!
C'MON DUSTER!
WHAT A FINISH! BUT IS IT ENOUGH TO MAKE THE TOP FIVE?
HEY, PAL! THAT WAS A HECK OF A RUN!
THANKS.
JETSTREAM, SIXTH PLACE! BUT WHAT A CLOSE ONE, PEOPLE...

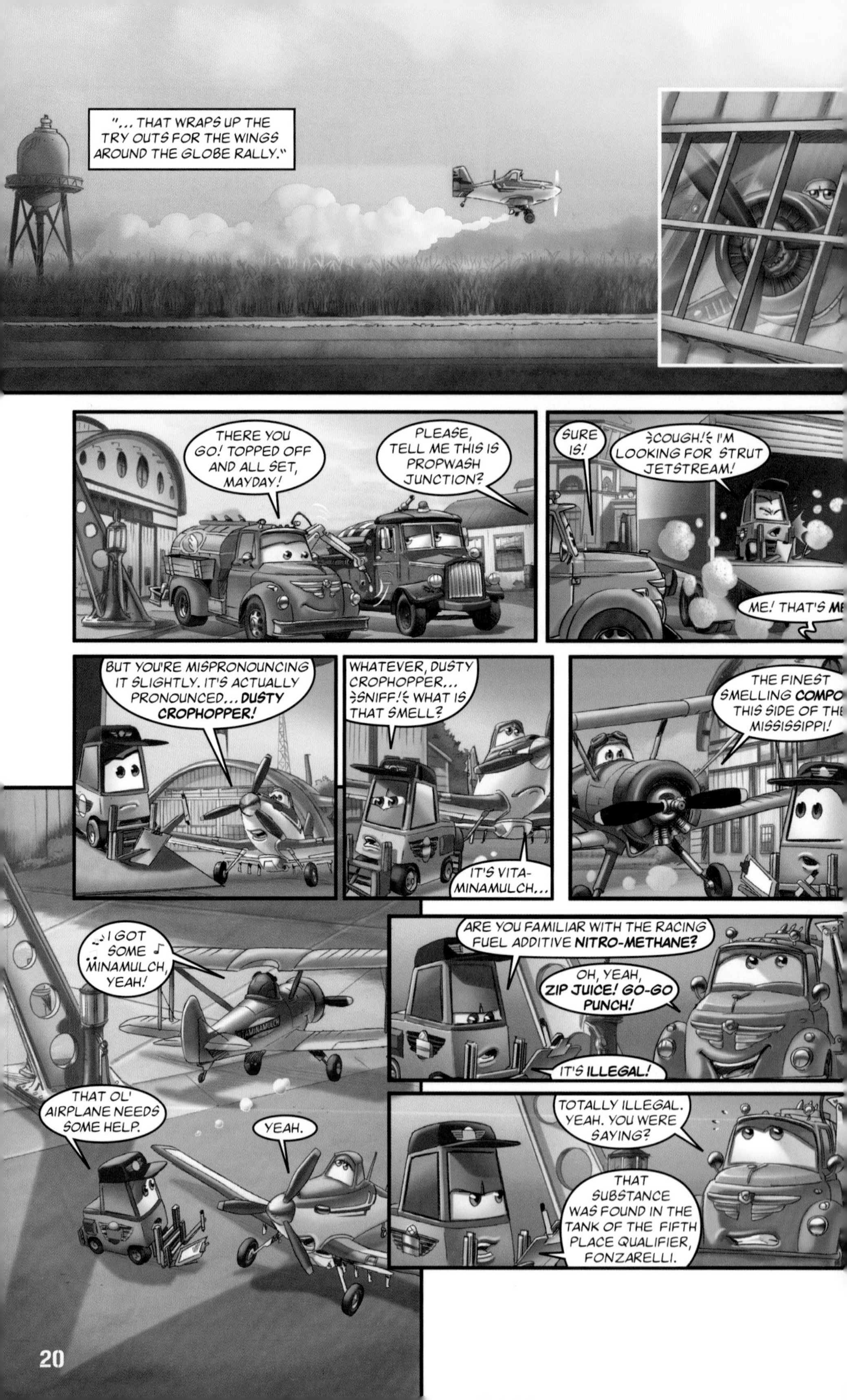
"... THAT WRAPS UP THE TRY OUTS FOR THE WINGS AROUND THE GLOBE RALLY."
THERE YOU GO! TOPPED OFF AND ALL SET, MAYDAY!
PLEASE, TELL ME THIS IS PROPWASH JUNCTION?
SURE IS!
COUGH! I'M LOOKING FOR STRUT JETSTREAM!
ME! THAT'S ME
BUT YOU'RE MISPRONOUNCING IT SLIGHTLY. IT'S ACTUALLY PRONOUNCED... DUSTY CROPHOPPER!
WHATEVER, DUSTY CROPHOPPER... SNIFF! WHAT IS THAT SMELL?
IT'S VITA-MINAMULCH...
THE FINEST SMELLING COMPO THIS SIDE OF THE MISSISSIPPI!
I GOT SOME MINAMULCH, YEAH!
ARE YOU FAMILIAR WITH THE RACING FUEL ADDITIVE NITRO-METHANE?
OH, YEAH, ZIP JUICE! GO-GO PUNCH!
IT'S ILLEGAL!
THAT OL' AIRPLANE NEEDS SOME HELP.
YEAH.
TOTALLY ILLEGAL. YEAH. YOU WERE SAYING?
THAT SUBSTANCE WAS FOUND IN THE TANK OF THE FIFTH PLACE QUALIFIER, FONZARELLI.

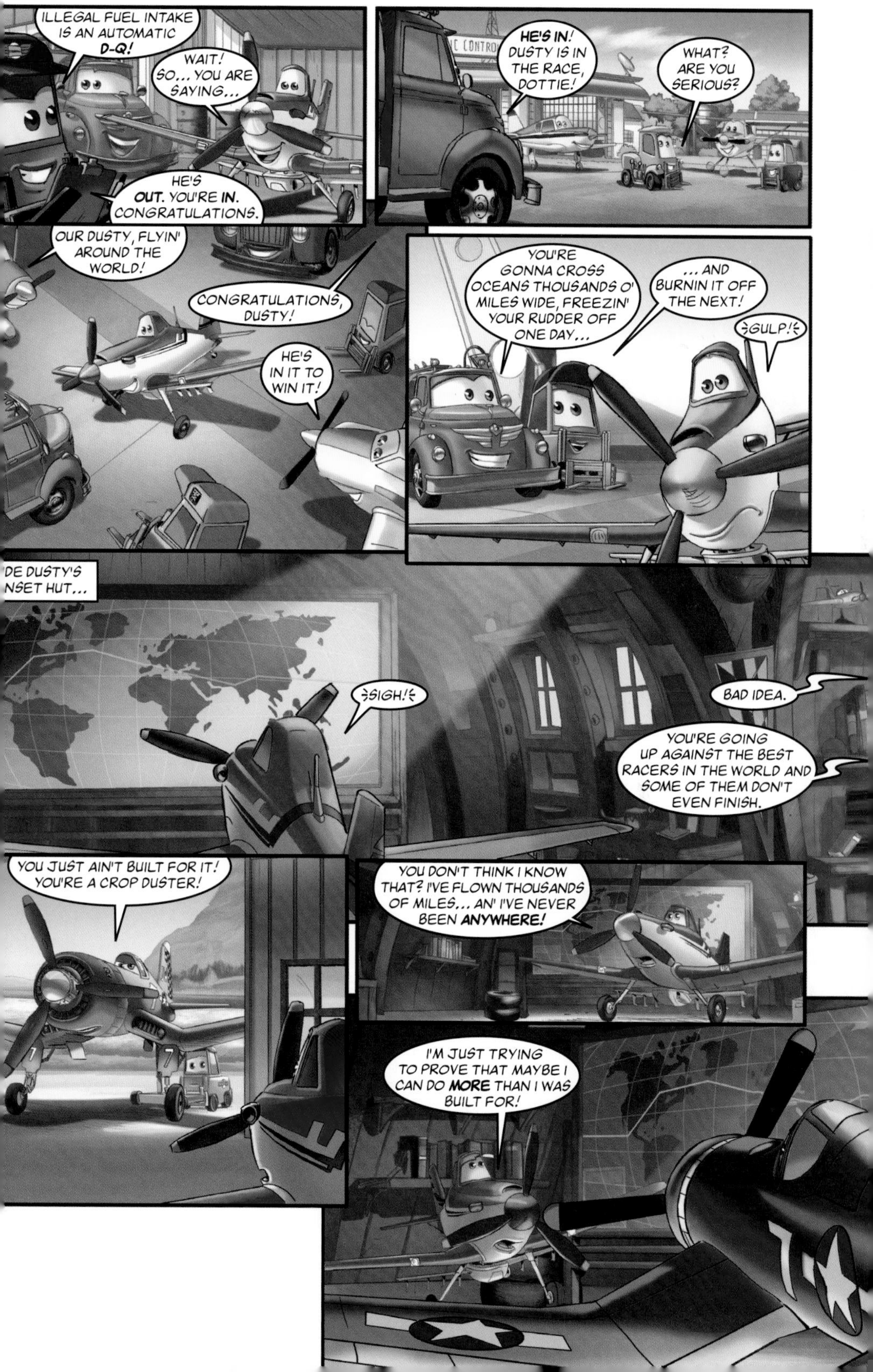
ILLEGAL FUEL INTAKE IS AN AUTOMATIC D-Q!
WAIT! SO... YOU ARE SAYING...
HE'S OUT. YOU'RE IN. CONGRATULATIONS.
HE'S IN! DUSTY IS IN THE RACE, DOTTIE!
WHAT? ARE YOU SERIOUS?
OUR DUSTY, FLYIN' AROUND THE WORLD!
CONGRATULATIONS, DUSTY!
HE'S IN IT TO WIN IT!
YOU'RE GONNA CROSS OCEANS THOUSANDS O' MILES WIDE, FREEZIN' YOUR RUDDER OFF ONE DAY...
... AND BURNIN IT OFF THE NEXT!
GULP!
DE DUSTY'S NSET HUT...
SIGH!
BAD IDEA.
YOU'RE GOING UP AGAINST THE BEST RACERS IN THE WORLD AND SOME OF THEM DON'T EVEN FINISH.
YOU JUST AIN'T BUILT FOR IT! YOU'RE A CROP DUSTER!
YOU DON'T THINK I KNOW THAT? I'VE FLOWN THOUSANDS OF MILES... AN' I'VE NEVER BEEN ANYWHERE!
I'M JUST TRYING TO PROVE THAT MAYBE I CAN DO MORE THAN I WAS BUILT FOR!

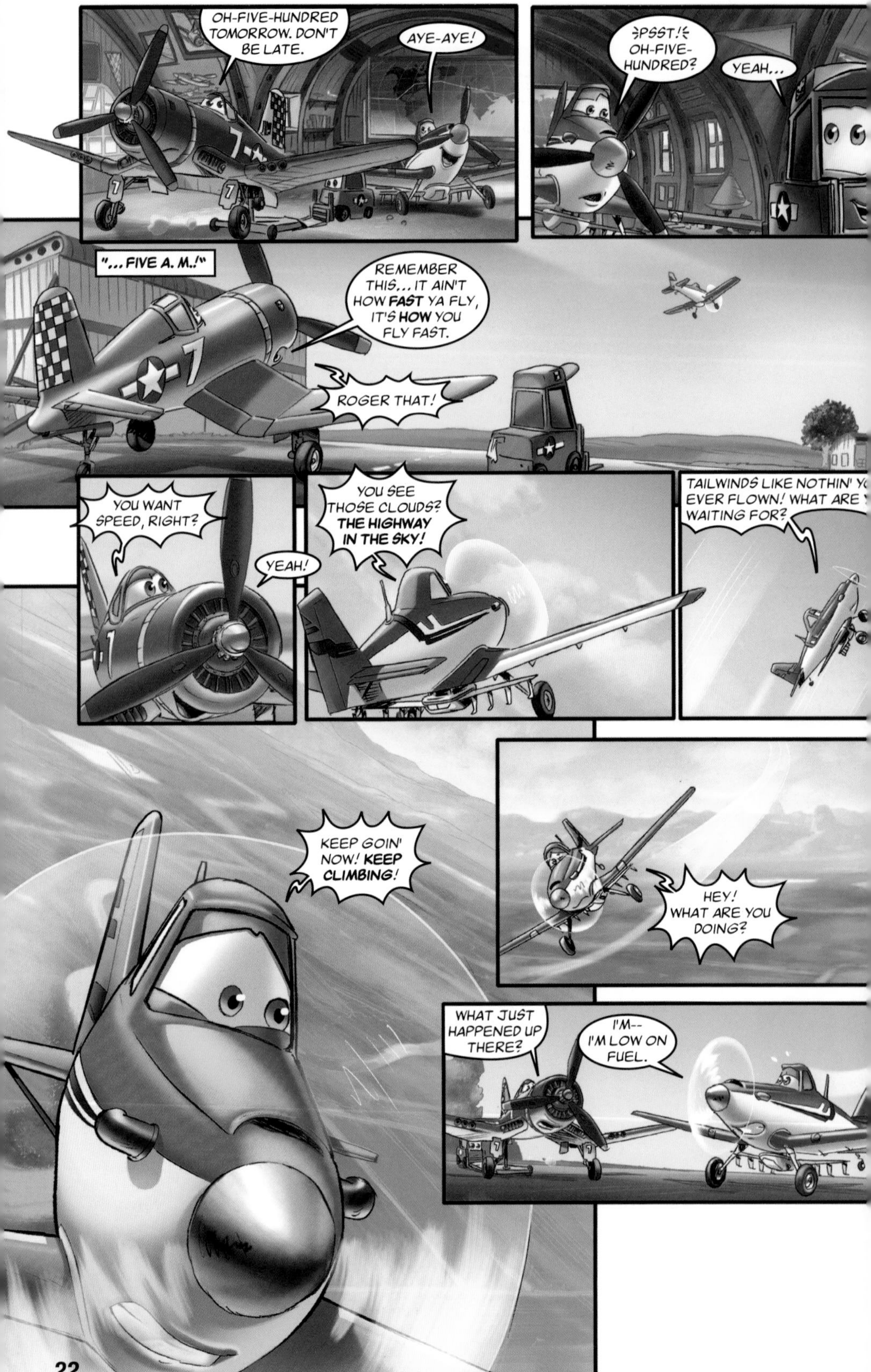
OH-FIVE-HUNDRED TOMORROW. DON'T BE LATE.
AYE-AYE!
PSST! OH-FIVE-HUNDRED?
YEAH...
"...FIVE A. M.!"
REMEMBER THIS... IT AIN'T HOW FAST YA FLY, IT'S HOW YOU FLY FAST.
ROGER THAT!
YOU WANT SPEED, RIGHT?
YEAH!
YOU SEE THOSE CLOUDS? THE HIGHWAY IN THE SKY!
TAILWINDS LIKE NOTHIN' YOU EVER FLOWN! WHAT ARE YOU WAITING FOR?
KEEP GOIN' NOW! KEEP CLIMBING!
HEY! WHAT ARE YOU DOING?
WHAT JUST HAPPENED UP THERE?
I'M-- I'M LOW ON FUEL.

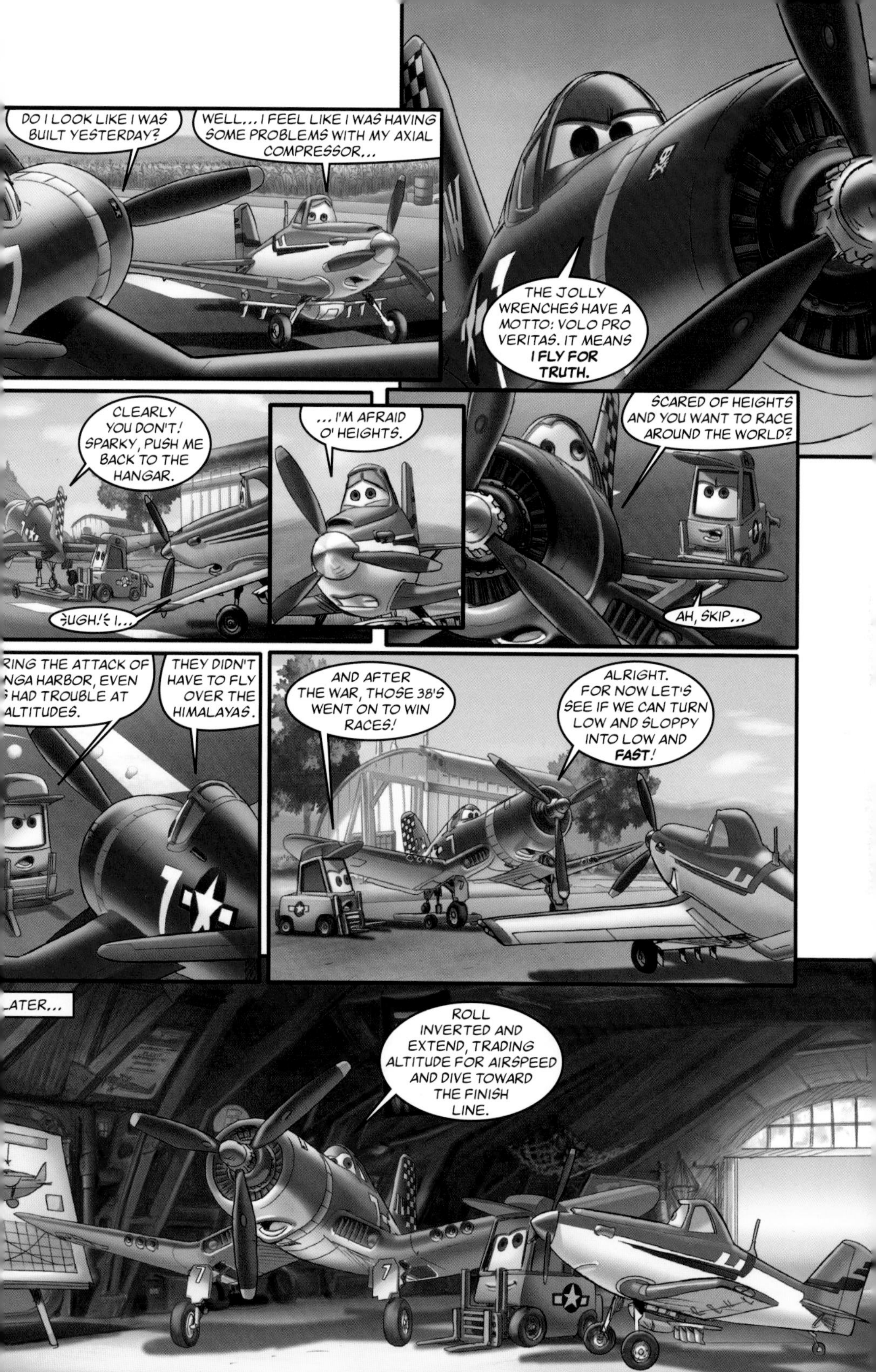
DO I LOOK LIKE I WAS BUILT YESTERDAY?
WELL... I FEEL LIKE I WAS HAVING SOME PROBLEMS WITH MY AXIAL COMPRESSOR...
THE JOLLY WRENCHES HAVE A MOTTO: VOLO PRO VERITAS. IT MEANS **I FLY FOR TRUTH.**
CLEARLY YOU DON'T! SPARKY, PUSH ME BACK TO THE HANGAR.
UGH! I...
...I'M AFRAID O' HEIGHTS.
SCARED OF HEIGHTS AND YOU WANT TO RACE AROUND THE WORLD?
AH, SKIP...
RING THE ATTACK OF
NGA HARBOR, EVEN
HAD TROUBLE AT
ALTITUDES.
THEY DIDN'T HAVE TO FLY OVER THE HIMALAYAS.
AND AFTER THE WAR, THOSE 38'S WENT ON TO WIN RACES!
ALRIGHT. FOR NOW LET'S SEE IF WE CAN TURN LOW AND SLOPPY INTO LOW AND **FAST**!
LATER...
ROLL INVERTED AND EXTEND, TRADING ALTITUDE FOR AIRSPEED AND DIVE TOWARD THE FINISH LINE.

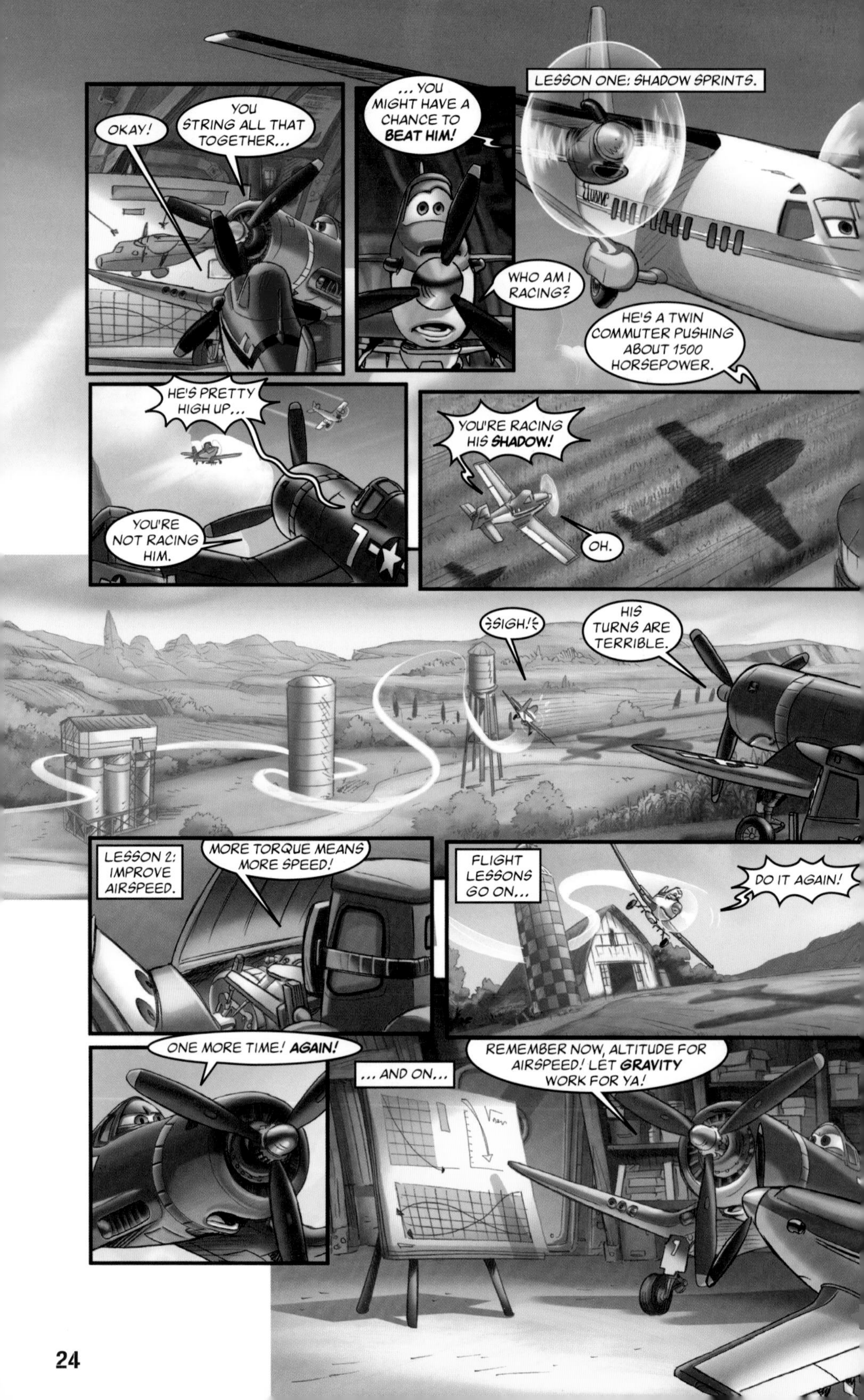
OKAY!
YOU STRING ALL THAT TOGETHER...
... YOU MIGHT HAVE A CHANCE TO BEAT HIM!
WHO AM I RACING?
LESSON ONE: SHADOW SPRINTS.
HE'S A TWIN COMMUTER PUSHING ABOUT 1500 HORSEPOWER.
HE'S PRETTY HIGH UP...
YOU'RE NOT RACING HIM.
YOU'RE RACING HIS SHADOW!
OH.
SIGH!
HIS TURNS ARE TERRIBLE.
LESSON 2: IMPROVE AIRSPEED.
MORE TORQUE MEANS MORE SPEED!
FLIGHT LESSONS GO ON...
DO IT AGAIN!
ONE MORE TIME! AGAIN!
... AND ON...
REMEMBER NOW, ALTITUDE FOR AIRSPEED! LET GRAVITY WORK FOR YA!

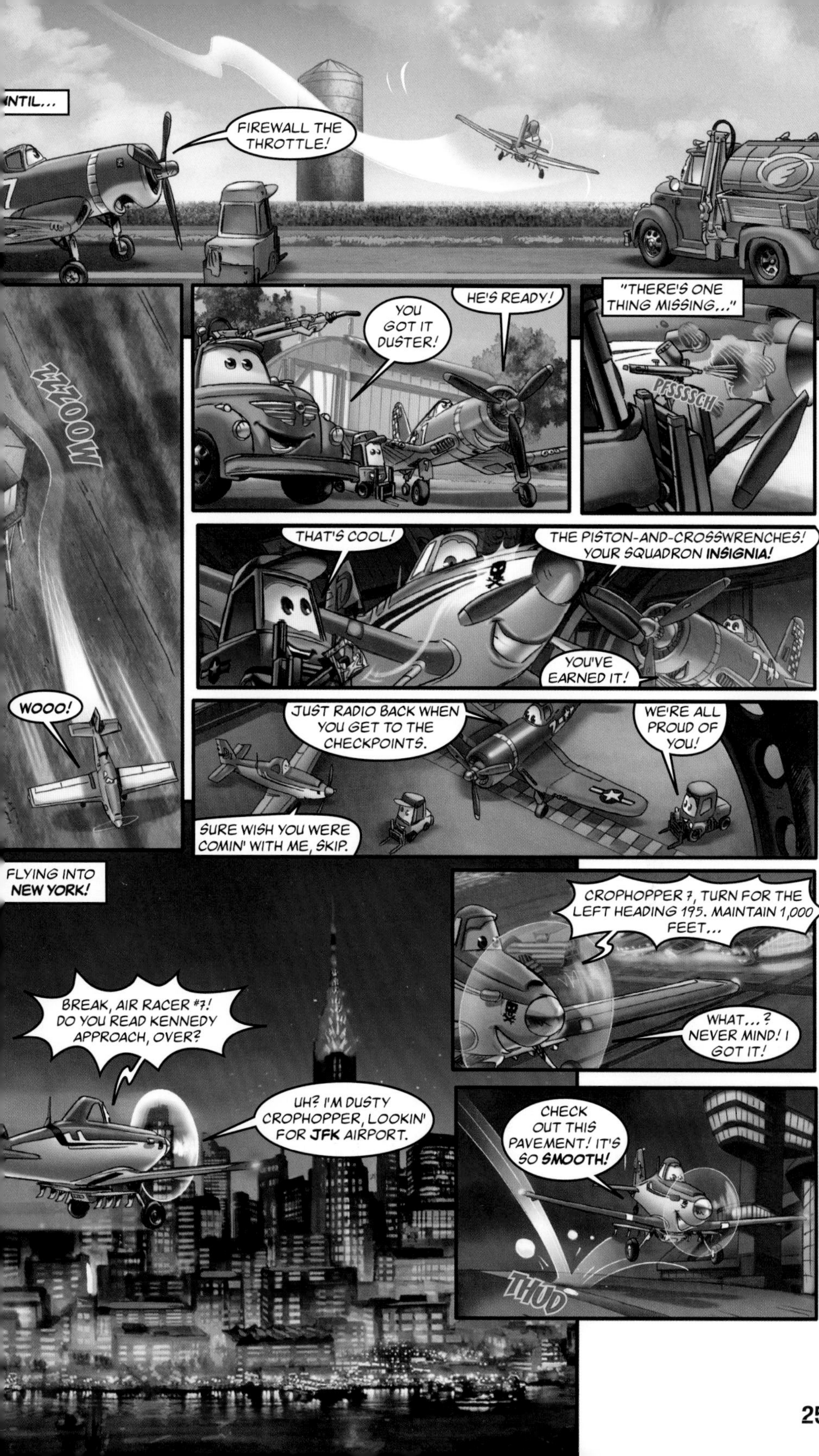
INTIL...
FIREWALL THE THROTTLE!
WZOOM
YOU GOT IT DUSTER!
HE'S READY!
"THERE'S ONE THING MISSING..."
PFSSSSCH
THAT'S COOL!
THE PISTON-AND-CROSSWRENCHES! YOUR SQUADRON INSIGNIA!
YOU'VE EARNED IT!
WOOO!
JUST RADIO BACK WHEN YOU GET TO THE CHECKPOINTS.
WE'RE ALL PROUD OF YOU!
SURE WISH YOU WERE COMIN' WITH ME, SKIP.
FLYING INTO NEW YORK!
BREAK, AIR RACER #7! DO YOU READ KENNEDY APPROACH, OVER?
UH? I'M DUSTY CROPHOPPER, LOOKIN' FOR JFK AIRPORT.
CROPHOPPER 7, TURN FOR THE LEFT HEADING 195. MAINTAIN 1,000 FEET...
WHAT...? NEVER MIND! I GOT IT!
CHECK OUT THIS PAVEMENT! IT'S SO SMOOTH!
THUD

EXCUSE ME. I'M LOOKING FOR PIT ROW...

YOU MIND? I'M WORKIN' HERE!

STRAIGHT AHEAD AND TO YOUR LEFT.

WELCOME RACERS

OH!

WELL, LOOKIE WHO'S HERE!

YOUR TENT'S THE LAST ONE ON THE LEFT.

THANKS!

WOW! BULLDOG, FROM THE EUROPEAN CUP!

I SAW YOU DO THIS HIGH-G VERTICAL TURN! HOW DID YOU DO THAT?

WHY DON'T I TELL YOU ALL MY RACING SECRETS?

THIS IS A COMPETITION! EVERY PLANE FOR HIMSELF!

YEAH,... SURE.

HEY! YOU ARE PAN-ASIAN CHAMPION AND MUMBAI CUP RECORD-HOLDER ISHANI!

MOST PEOPLE JUST CALL ME ISHANI.

I'M DUSTY! I... I MEAN, MY NAME IS DUSTY!

I'M NOT ACTUALLY DUSTY! I'M... QUITE CLEAN.

IT IS VERY NICE TO MEET YOU, QUITE CLEAN DUSTY.

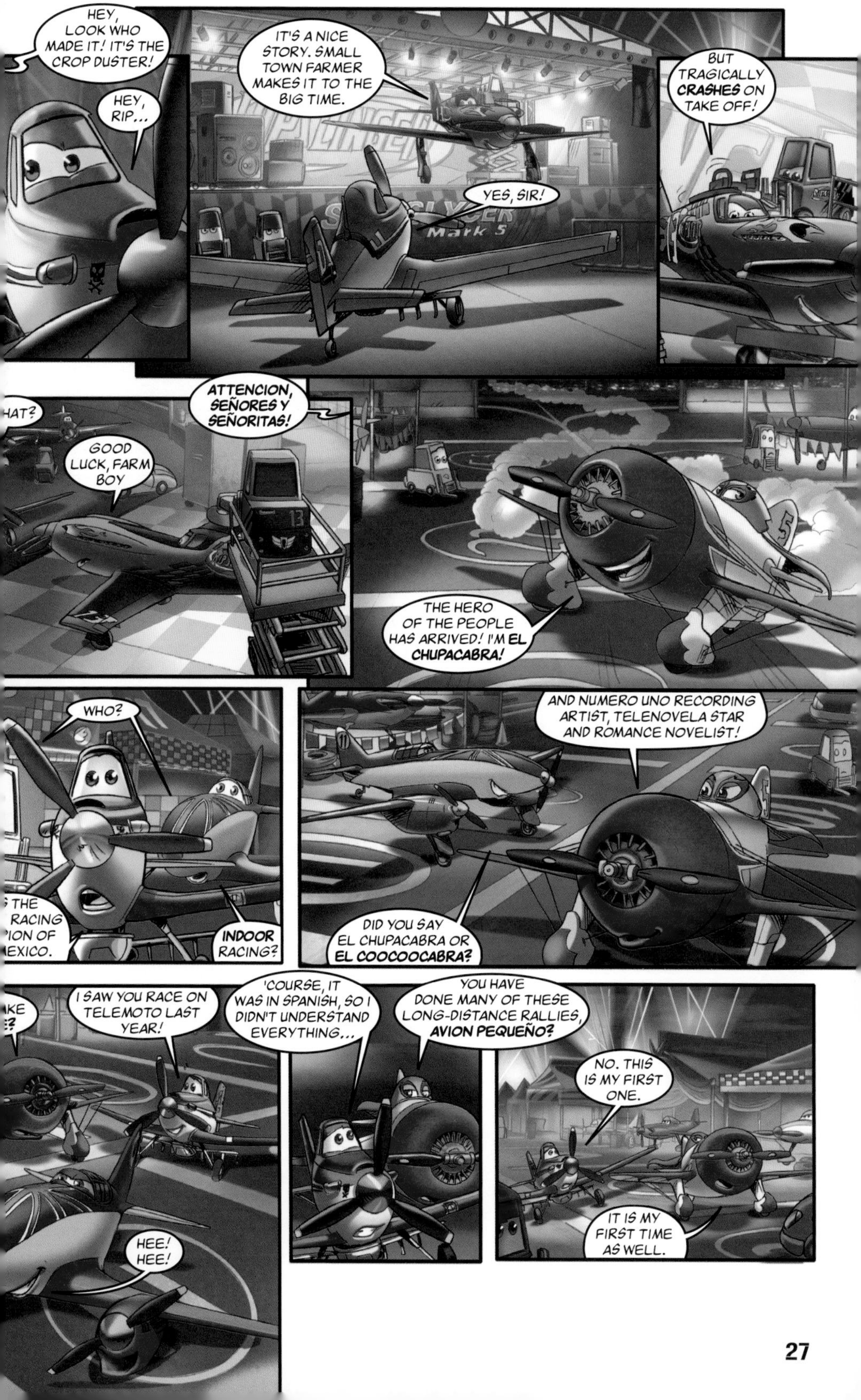

HEY, LOOK WHO MADE IT! IT'S THE CROP DUSTER!
HEY, RIP...
IT'S A NICE STORY. SMALL TOWN FARMER MAKES IT TO THE BIG TIME.
YES, SIR!
BUT TRAGICALLY CRASHES ON TAKE OFF!
HAT?
GOOD LUCK, FARM BOY
ATTENCION, SEÑORES Y SEÑORITAS!
THE HERO OF THE PEOPLE HAS ARRIVED! I'M EL CHUPACABRA!
WHO?
THE RACING PION OF EXICO.
INDOOR RACING?
AND NUMERO UNO RECORDING ARTIST, TELENOVELA STAR AND ROMANCE NOVELIST!
DID YOU SAY EL CHUPACABRA OR EL COOCOOCABRA?
AKE
I SAW YOU RACE ON TELEMOTO LAST YEAR!
HEE! HEE!
'COURSE, IT WAS IN SPANISH, SO I DIDN'T UNDERSTAND EVERYTHING...
YOU HAVE DONE MANY OF THESE LONG-DISTANCE RALLIES, AVION PEQUEÑO?
NO. THIS IS MY FIRST ONE.
IT IS MY FIRST TIME AS WELL.

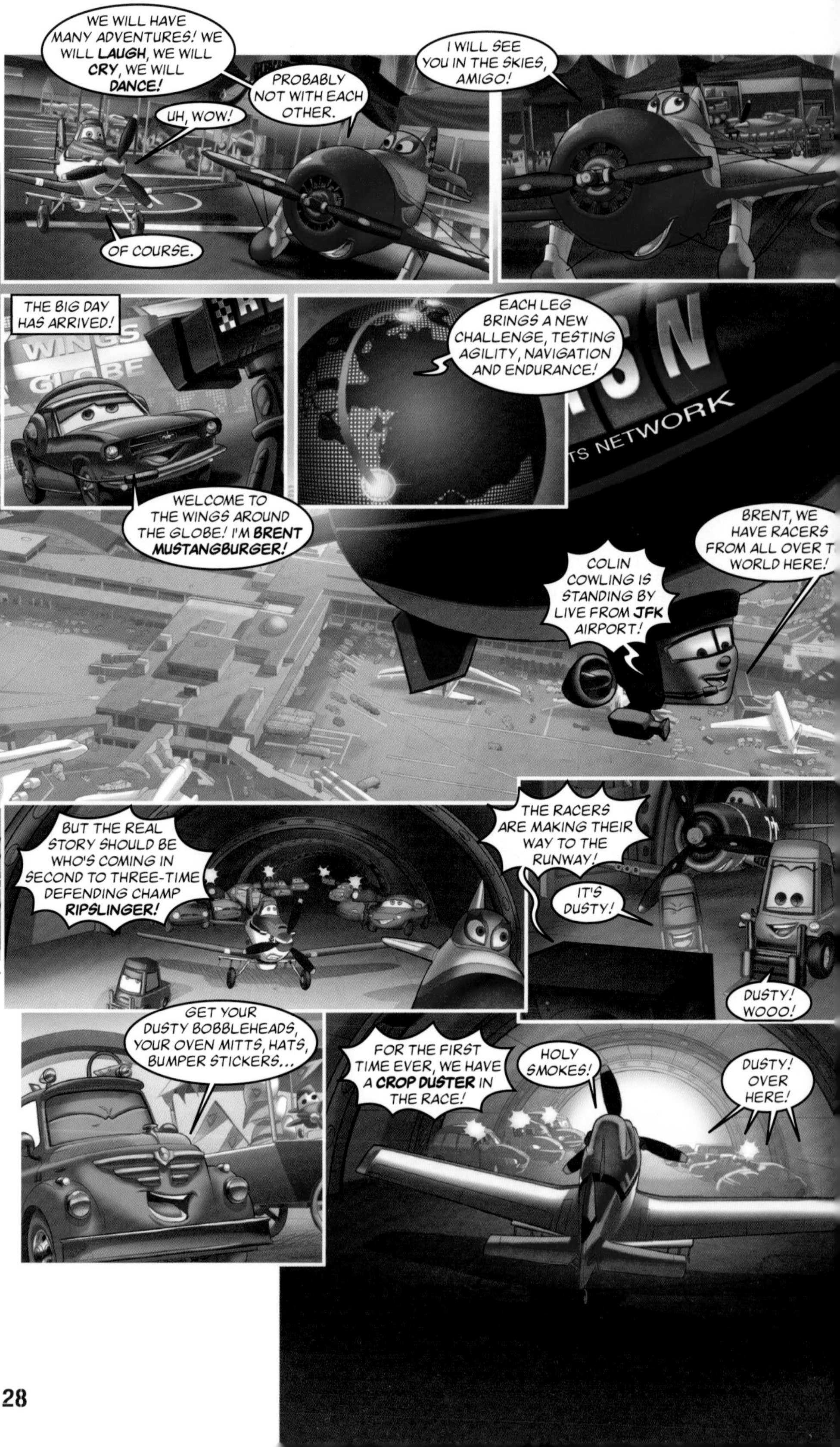

WE WILL HAVE MANY ADVENTURES! WE WILL **LAUGH**, WE WILL **CRY**, WE WILL **DANCE!**
UH, WOW!
PROBABLY NOT WITH EACH OTHER.
OF COURSE.
I WILL SEE YOU IN THE SKIES, AMIGO!
THE BIG DAY HAS ARRIVED!
EACH LEG BRINGS A NEW CHALLENGE, TESTING AGILITY, NAVIGATION AND ENDURANCE!
WELCOME TO THE WINGS AROUND THE GLOBE! I'M **BRENT MUSTANGBURGER!**
COLIN COWLING IS STANDING BY LIVE FROM **JFK** AIRPORT!
BRENT, WE HAVE RACERS FROM ALL OVER T WORLD HERE!
BUT THE REAL STORY SHOULD BE WHO'S COMING IN SECOND TO THREE-TIME DEFENDING CHAMP **RIPSLINGER!**
THE RACERS ARE MAKING THEIR WAY TO THE RUNWAY!
IT'S DUSTY!
DUSTY! WOOO!
GET YOUR DUSTY BOBBLEHEADS, YOUR OVEN MITTS, HATS, BUMPER STICKERS...
FOR THE FIRST TIME EVER, WE HAVE A **CROP DUSTER** IN THE RACE!
HOLY SMOKES!
DUSTY! OVER HERE!

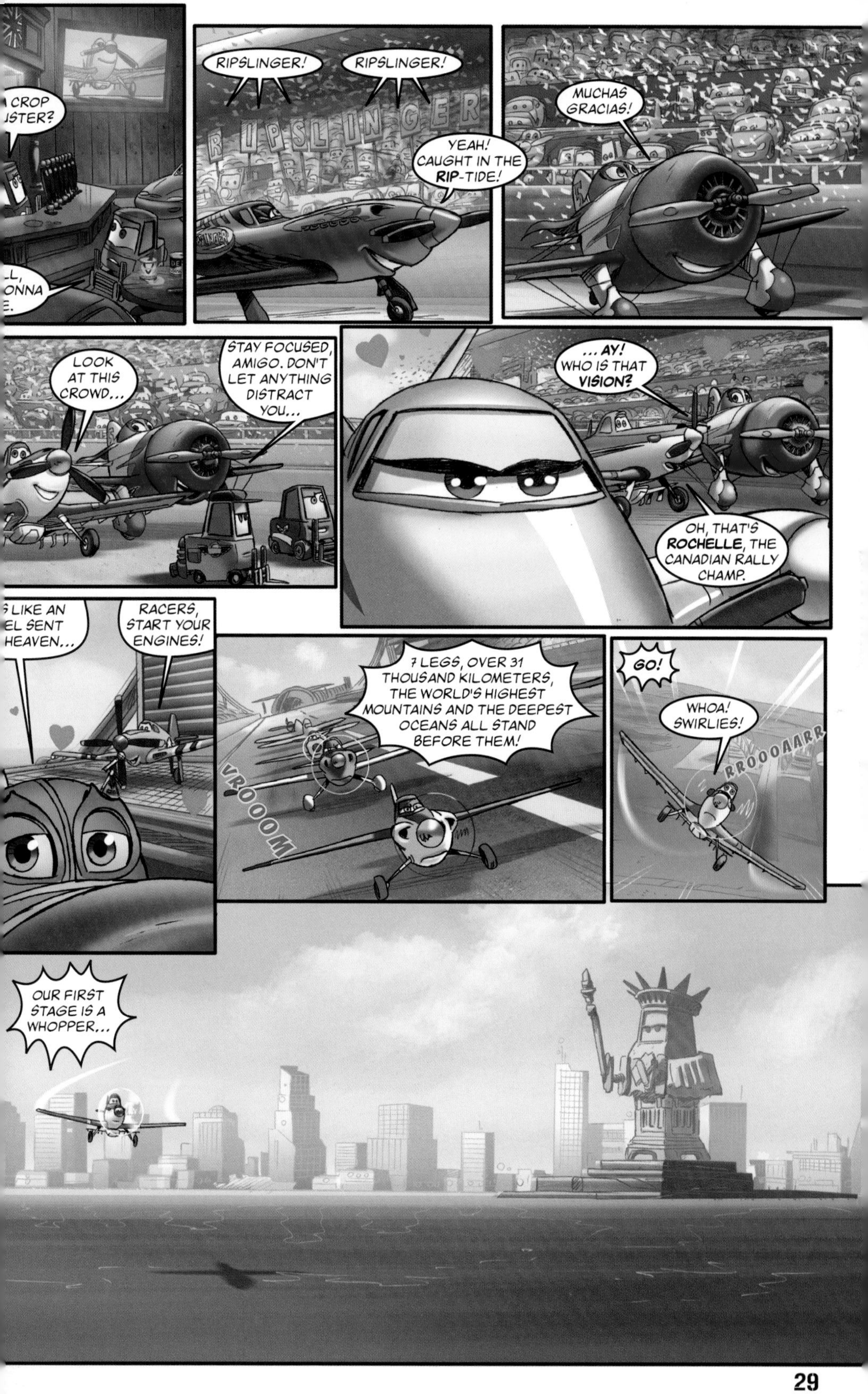
CROP
RIPSLINGER!
RIPSLINGER!
YEAH! CAUGHT IN THE RIP-TIDE!
MUCHAS GRACIAS!
LOOK AT THIS CROWD...
STAY FOCUSED, AMIGO. DON'T LET ANYTHING DISTRACT YOU...
...AY! WHO IS THAT VISION?
OH, THAT'S ROCHELLE, THE CANADIAN RALLY CHAMP.
LIKE AN
SENT
HEAVEN...
RACERS, START YOUR ENGINES!
7 LEGS, OVER 31 THOUSAND KILOMETERS, THE WORLD'S HIGHEST MOUNTAINS AND THE DEEPEST OCEANS ALL STAND BEFORE THEM!
VROOOM
GO!
WHOA! SWIRLIES!
RROOOAARR
OUR FIRST STAGE IS A WHOPPER...

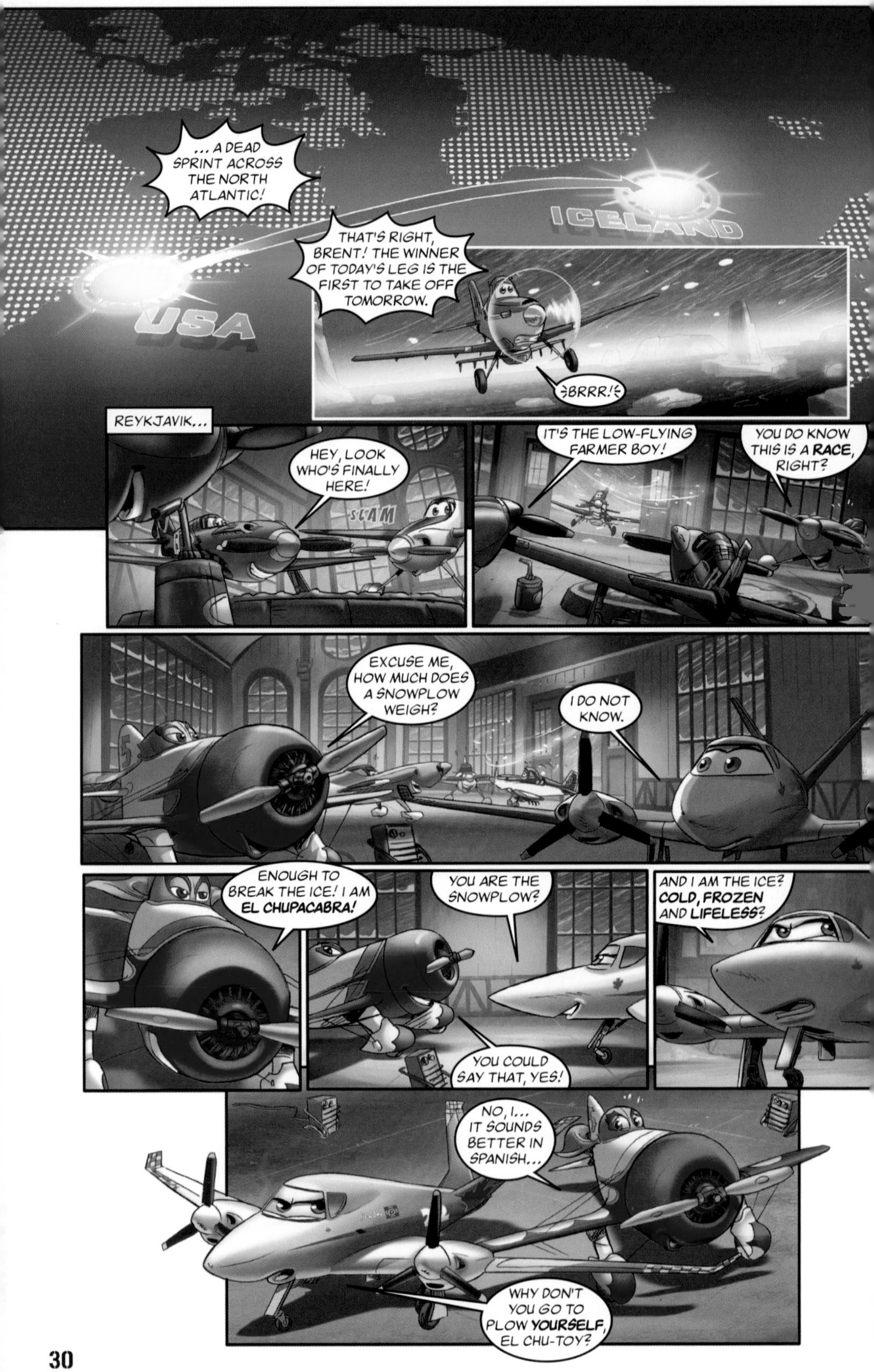
... A DEAD SPRINT ACROSS THE NORTH ATLANTIC!
ICELAND
USA
THAT'S RIGHT, BRENT! THE WINNER OF TODAY'S LEG IS THE FIRST TO TAKE OFF TOMORROW.
BRRR!
REYKJAVIK...
HEY, LOOK WHO'S FINALLY HERE!
SLAM
IT'S THE LOW-FLYING FARMER BOY!
YOU DO KNOW THIS IS A **RACE**, RIGHT?
EXCUSE ME, HOW MUCH DOES A SNOWPLOW WEIGH?
I DO NOT KNOW.
ENOUGH TO BREAK THE ICE! I AM **EL CHUPACABRA!**
YOU ARE THE SNOWPLOW?
YOU COULD SAY THAT, YES!
AND I AM THE ICE? **COLD, FROZEN** AND **LIFELESS?**
NO, I... IT SOUNDS BETTER IN SPANISH...
WHY DON'T YOU GO TO PLOW **YOURSELF**, EL CHU-TOY?

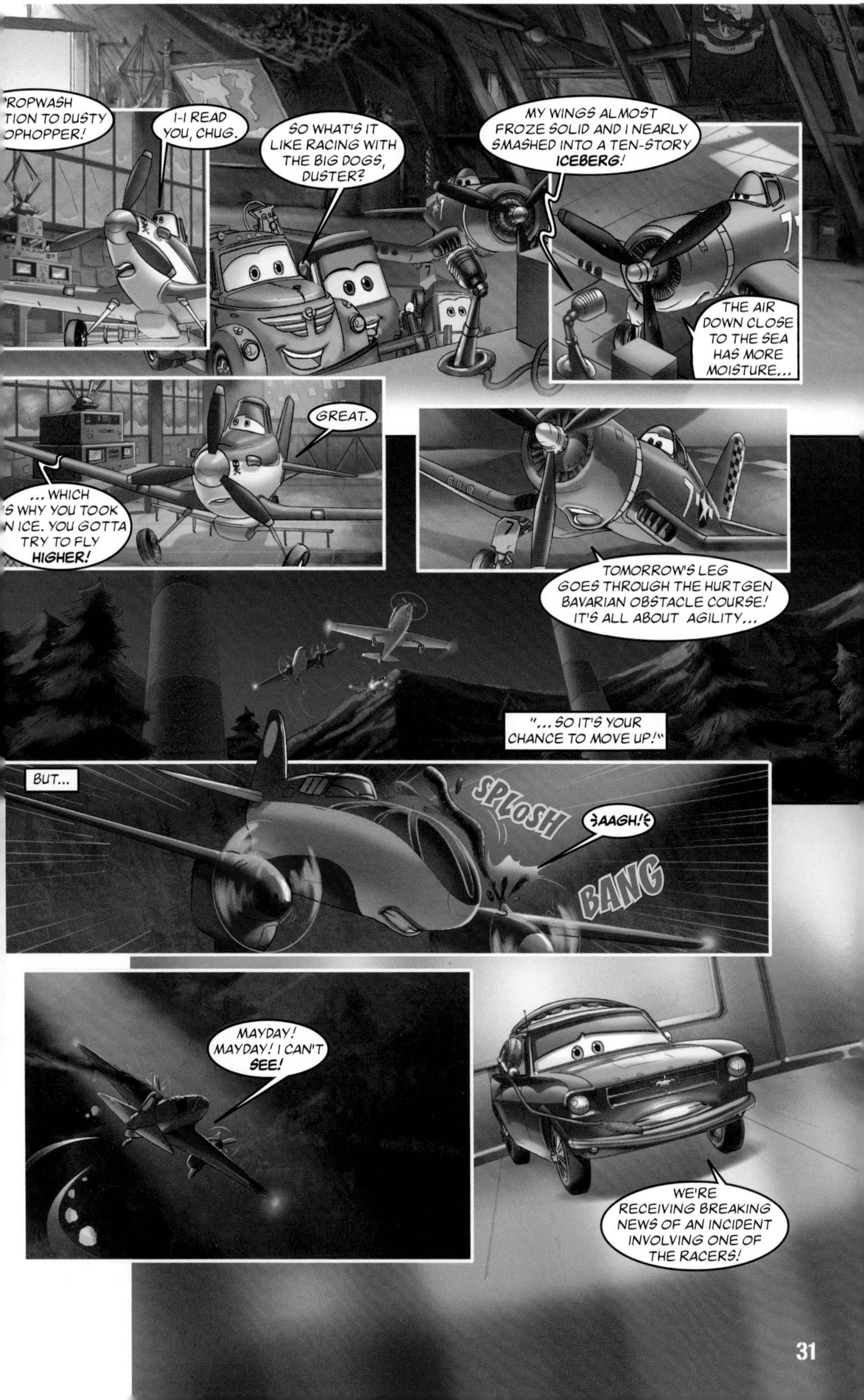

PROPWASH
TION TO DUSTY
OPHOPPER!
I-I READ YOU, CHUG.
SO WHAT'S IT LIKE RACING WITH THE BIG DOGS, DUSTER?
MY WINGS ALMOST FROZE SOLID AND I NEARLY SMASHED INTO A TEN-STORY ICEBERG!
THE AIR DOWN CLOSE TO THE SEA HAS MORE MOISTURE...
GREAT.
... WHICH
'S WHY YOU TOOK
N ICE. YOU GOTTA
TRY TO FLY HIGHER!
TOMORROW'S LEG GOES THROUGH THE HURTGEN BAVARIAN OBSTACLE COURSE! IT'S ALL ABOUT AGILITY...
"... SO IT'S YOUR CHANCE TO MOVE UP!"
BUT...
SPLOSH
AAGH!
BANG
MAYDAY! MAYDAY! I CAN'T SEE!
WE'RE RECEIVING BREAKING NEWS OF AN INCIDENT INVOLVING ONE OF THE RACERS!

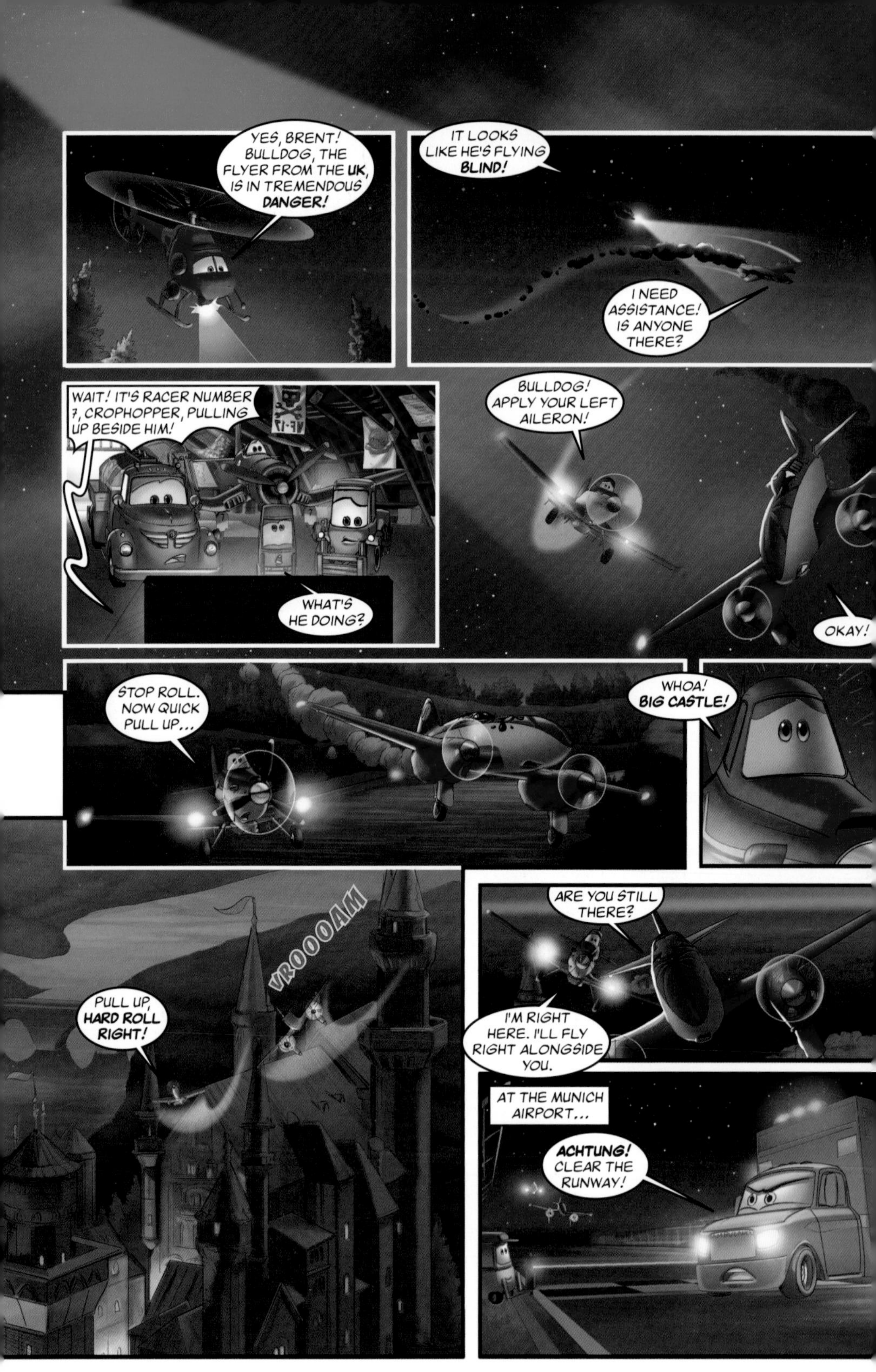
YES, BRENT! BULLDOG, THE FLYER FROM THE UK, IS IN TREMENDOUS DANGER!
IT LOOKS LIKE HE'S FLYING BLIND!
I NEED ASSISTANCE! IS ANYONE THERE?
WAIT! IT'S RACER NUMBER 7, CROPHOPPER, PULLING UP BESIDE HIM!
WHAT'S HE DOING?
BULLDOG! APPLY YOUR LEFT AILERON!
OKAY!
STOP ROLL. NOW QUICK PULL UP...
WHOA! BIG CASTLE!
PULL UP, HARD ROLL RIGHT!
VROOOOAM
ARE YOU STILL THERE?
I'M RIGHT HERE. I'LL FLY RIGHT ALONGSIDE YOU.
AT THE MUNICH AIRPORT...
ACHTUNG! CLEAR THE RUNWAY!

ADD POWER...
FLAPS DOWN...LANDING
GEAR DOWN!

MUNICH

DOWN AND
LOCKED!

CHIRP

CHIRP

...NKS FOR YOUR
HELP, I...

SPLAAASH

MUNICH

...YOU?
WHAT DID I TELL
YOU, BOY? EVERY
PLANE FOR
HIMSELF.

WHERE I COME
FROM, IF YOU SEE
SOMEONE FALLING
FROM THE SKY...

...HIS IS A COMPETITION!
...N YOU'RE DEAD LAST...
AND I OWE YOU
MY LIFE!

BULLDOG!

CAN WE
GET A FEW
WORDS?

I GOTTA SAY,
CROP DUSTER, YOU
ARE A NICE
GUY.

HEY,
THANKS,
RIP.

AND WE ALL KNOW
WHERE NICE GUYS
FINISH...HEH!
HEH!

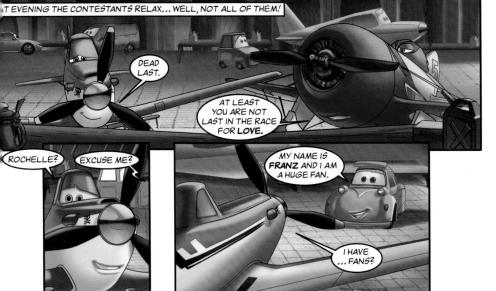

...T EVENING THE CONTESTANTS RELAX... WELL, NOT ALL OF THEM!

DEAD
LAST.

AT LEAST
YOU ARE NOT
LAST IN THE RACE
FOR LOVE.

ROCHELLE?

EXCUSE ME?

MY NAME IS
FRANZ AND I AM
A HUGE FAN.

I HAVE
...FANS?

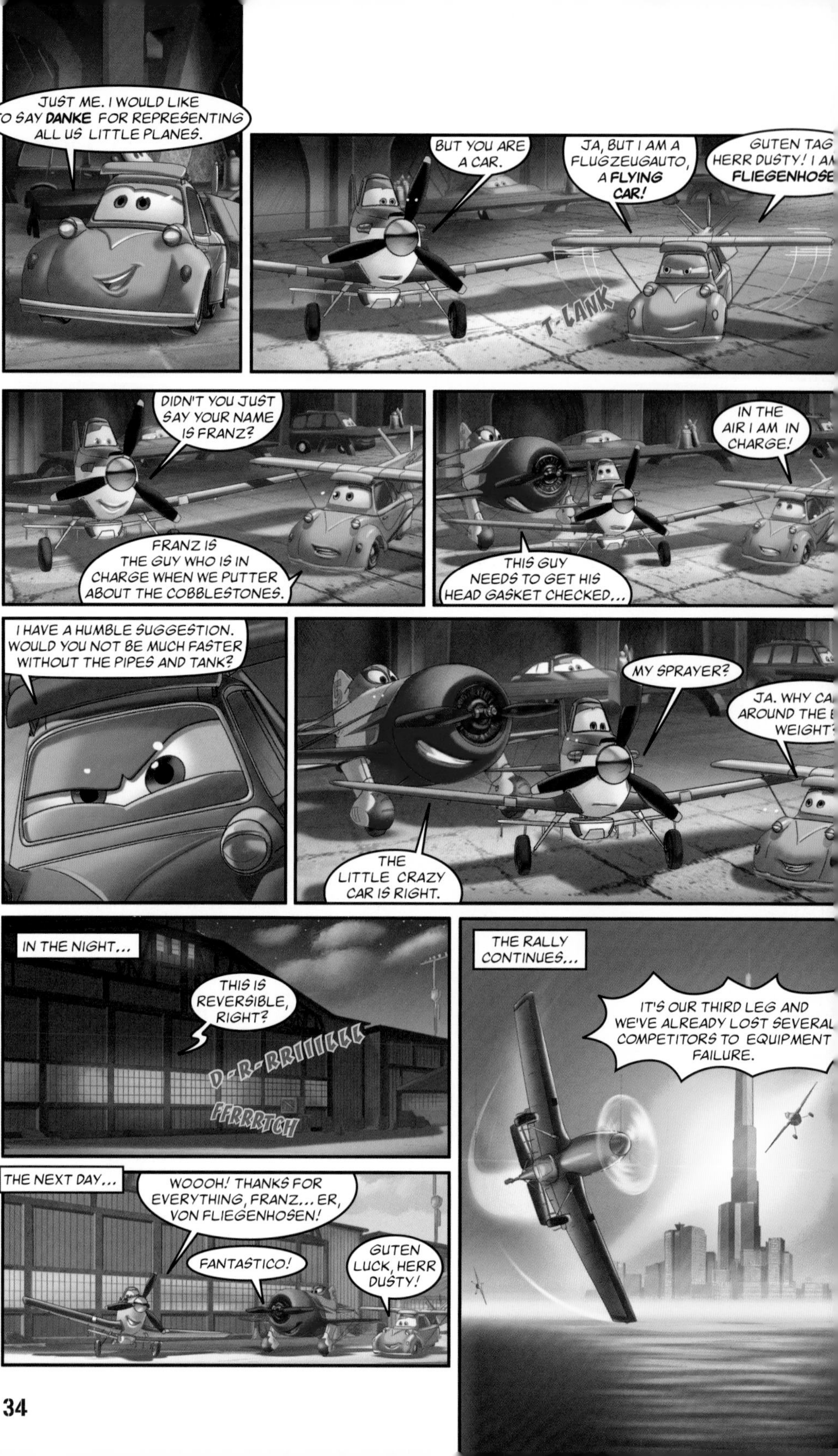
JUST ME. I WOULD LIKE TO SAY DANKE FOR REPRESENTING ALL US LITTLE PLANES.
BUT YOU ARE A CAR.
JA, BUT I AM A FLUGZEUGAUTO, A FLYING CAR!
GUTEN TAG HERR DUSTY! I AM FLIEGENHOSE
T-LANK
DIDN'T YOU JUST SAY YOUR NAME IS FRANZ?
FRANZ IS THE GUY WHO IS IN CHARGE WHEN WE PUTTER ABOUT THE COBBLESTONES.
IN THE AIR I AM IN CHARGE!
THIS GUY NEEDS TO GET HIS HEAD GASKET CHECKED...
I HAVE A HUMBLE SUGGESTION. WOULD YOU NOT BE MUCH FASTER WITHOUT THE PIPES AND TANK?
MY SPRAYER?
JA. WHY CA AROUND THE E WEIGHT?
THE LITTLE CRAZY CAR IS RIGHT.
IN THE NIGHT...
THIS IS REVERSIBLE, RIGHT?
D-R-RRIIIILLL
FFRRRTCH
THE NEXT DAY...
WOOOH! THANKS FOR EVERYTHING, FRANZ... ER, VON FLIEGENHOSEN!
FANTASTICO!
GUTEN LUCK, HERR DUSTY!
THE RALLY CONTINUES...
IT'S OUR THIRD LEG AND WE'VE ALREADY LOST SEVERAL COMPETITORS TO EQUIPMENT FAILURE.

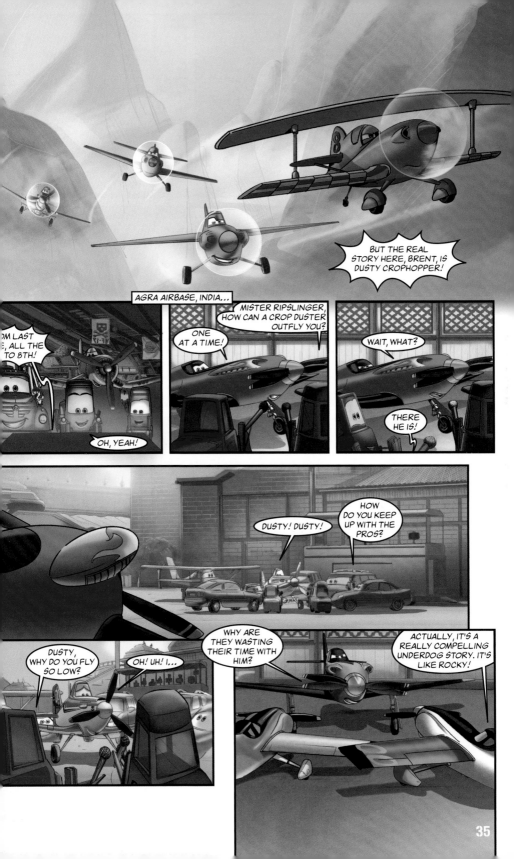

BUT THE REAL STORY HERE, BRENT, IS DUSTY CROPHOPPER!

AGRA AIRBASE, INDIA...

OM LAST ... ALL THE ... TO 8TH!

OH, YEAH!

MISTER RIPSLINGER, HOW CAN A CROP DUSTER OUTFLY YOU?

ONE AT A TIME!

WAIT, WHAT?

THERE HE IS!

DUSTY! DUSTY!

HOW DO YOU KEEP UP WITH THE PROS?

WHY ARE THEY WASTING THEIR TIME WITH HIM?

ACTUALLY, IT'S A REALLY COMPELLING UNDERDOG STORY. IT'S LIKE ROCKY!

DUSTY, WHY DO YOU FLY SO LOW?

OH! UH! I...

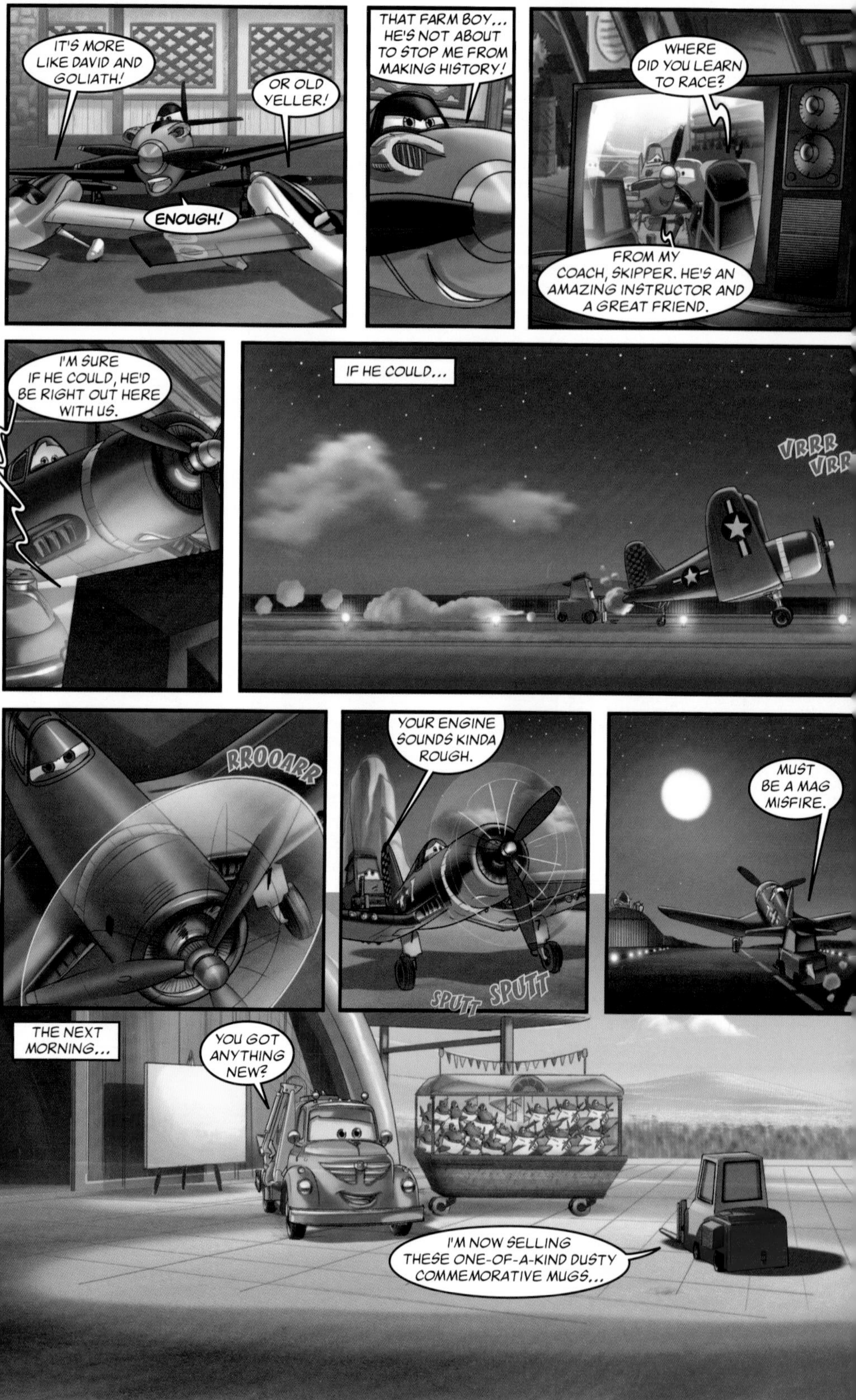
IT'S MORE LIKE DAVID AND GOLIATH!
OR OLD YELLER!
ENOUGH!
THAT FARM BOY... HE'S NOT ABOUT TO STOP ME FROM MAKING HISTORY!
WHERE DID YOU LEARN TO RACE?
FROM MY COACH, SKIPPER. HE'S AN AMAZING INSTRUCTOR AND A GREAT FRIEND.
I'M SURE IF HE COULD, HE'D BE RIGHT OUT HERE WITH US.
IF HE COULD...
VRRR VRR
RROOARR
YOUR ENGINE SOUNDS KINDA ROUGH.
SPUTT SPUTT
MUST BE A MAG MISFIRE.
THE NEXT MORNING...
YOU GOT ANYTHING NEW?
I'M NOW SELLING THESE ONE-OF-A-KIND DUSTY COMMEMORATIVE MUGS...

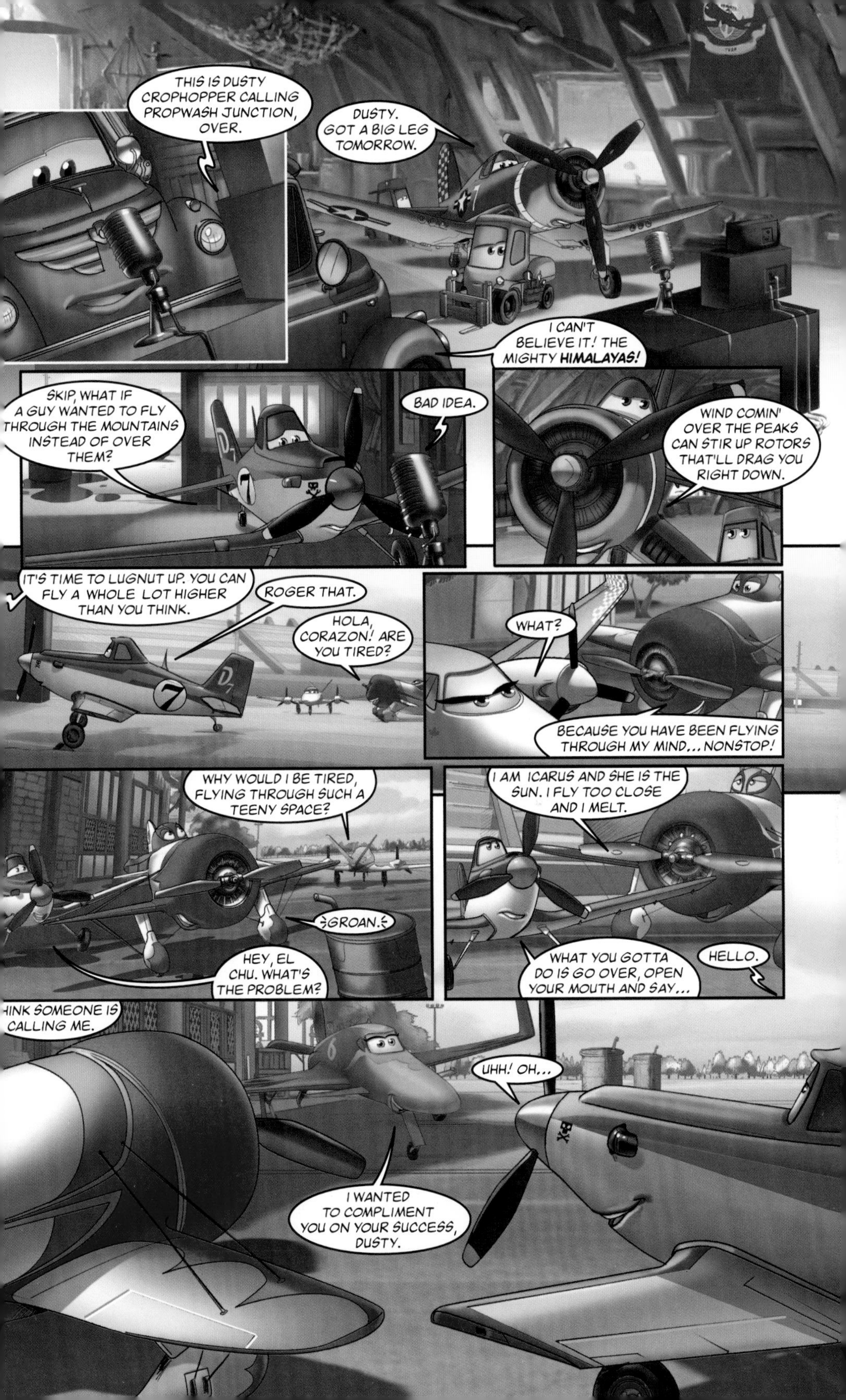
THIS IS DUSTY CROPHOPPER CALLING PROPWASH JUNCTION, OVER.
DUSTY. GOT A BIG LEG TOMORROW.
I CAN'T BELIEVE IT! THE MIGHTY HIMALAYAS!
SKIP, WHAT IF A GUY WANTED TO FLY THROUGH THE MOUNTAINS INSTEAD OF OVER THEM?
BAD IDEA.
WIND COMIN' OVER THE PEAKS CAN STIR UP ROTORS THAT'LL DRAG YOU RIGHT DOWN.
IT'S TIME TO LUGNUT UP. YOU CAN FLY A WHOLE LOT HIGHER THAN YOU THINK.
ROGER THAT.
HOLA, CORAZON! ARE YOU TIRED?
WHAT?
BECAUSE YOU HAVE BEEN FLYING THROUGH MY MIND... NONSTOP!
WHY WOULD I BE TIRED, FLYING THROUGH SUCH A TEENY SPACE?
GROAN.
HEY, EL CHU. WHAT'S THE PROBLEM?
I AM ICARUS AND SHE IS THE SUN. I FLY TOO CLOSE AND I MELT.
WHAT YOU GOTTA DO IS GO OVER, OPEN YOUR MOUTH AND SAY...
HELLO.
HINK SOMEONE IS CALLING ME.
UHH! OH...
I WANTED TO COMPLIMENT YOU ON YOUR SUCCESS, DUSTY.

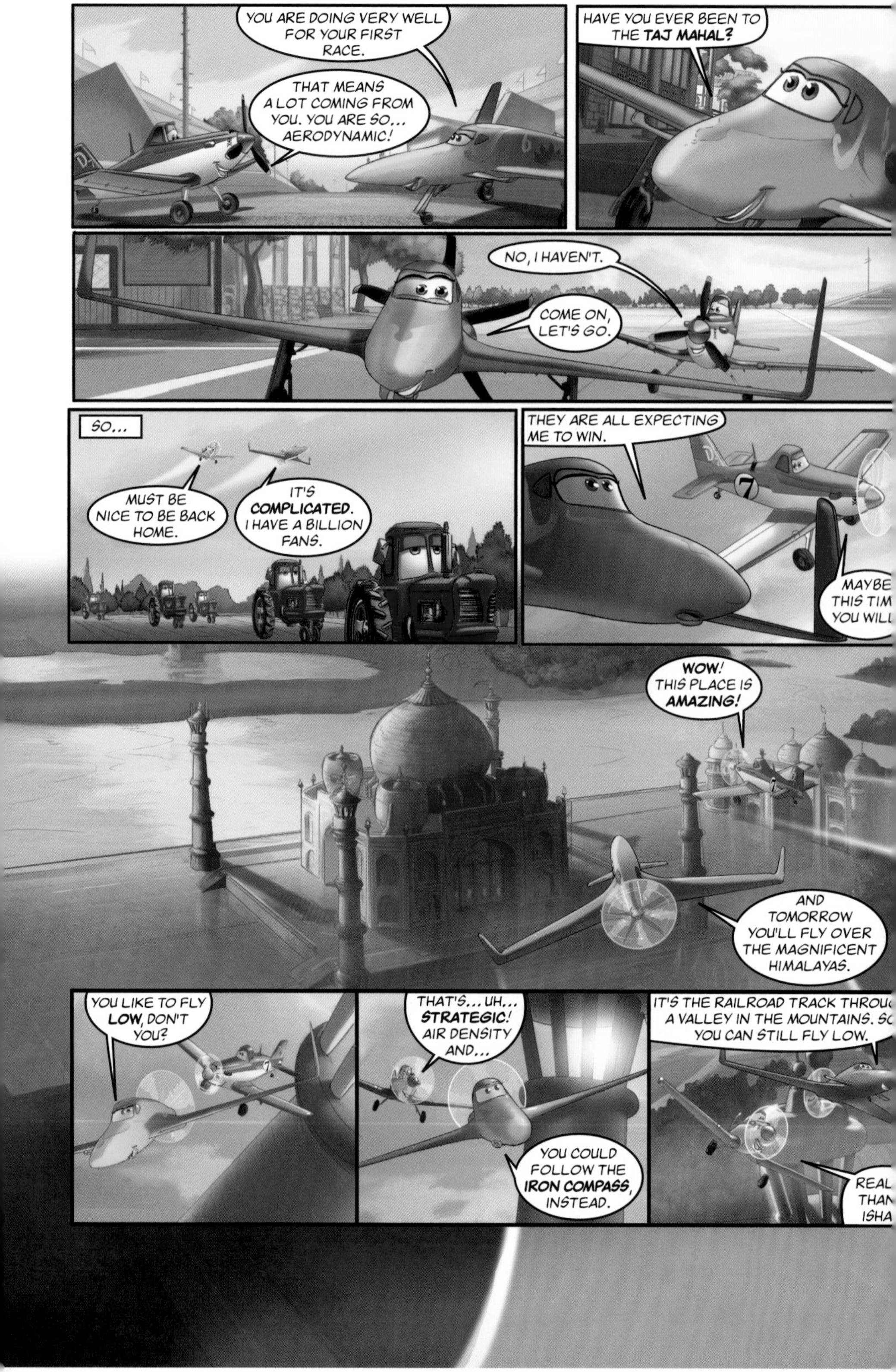
YOU ARE DOING VERY WELL FOR YOUR FIRST RACE.
THAT MEANS A LOT COMING FROM YOU. YOU ARE SO... AERODYNAMIC!
HAVE YOU EVER BEEN TO THE TAJ MAHAL?
NO, I HAVEN'T.
COME ON, LET'S GO.
SO...
MUST BE NICE TO BE BACK HOME.
IT'S COMPLICATED. I HAVE A BILLION FANS.
THEY ARE ALL EXPECTING ME TO WIN.
WOW! THIS PLACE IS AMAZING!
AND TOMORROW YOU'LL FLY OVER THE MAGNIFICENT HIMALAYAS.
YOU LIKE TO FLY LOW, DON'T YOU?
THAT'S... UH... STRATEGIC! AIR DENSITY AND...
YOU COULD FOLLOW THE IRON COMPASS, INSTEAD.

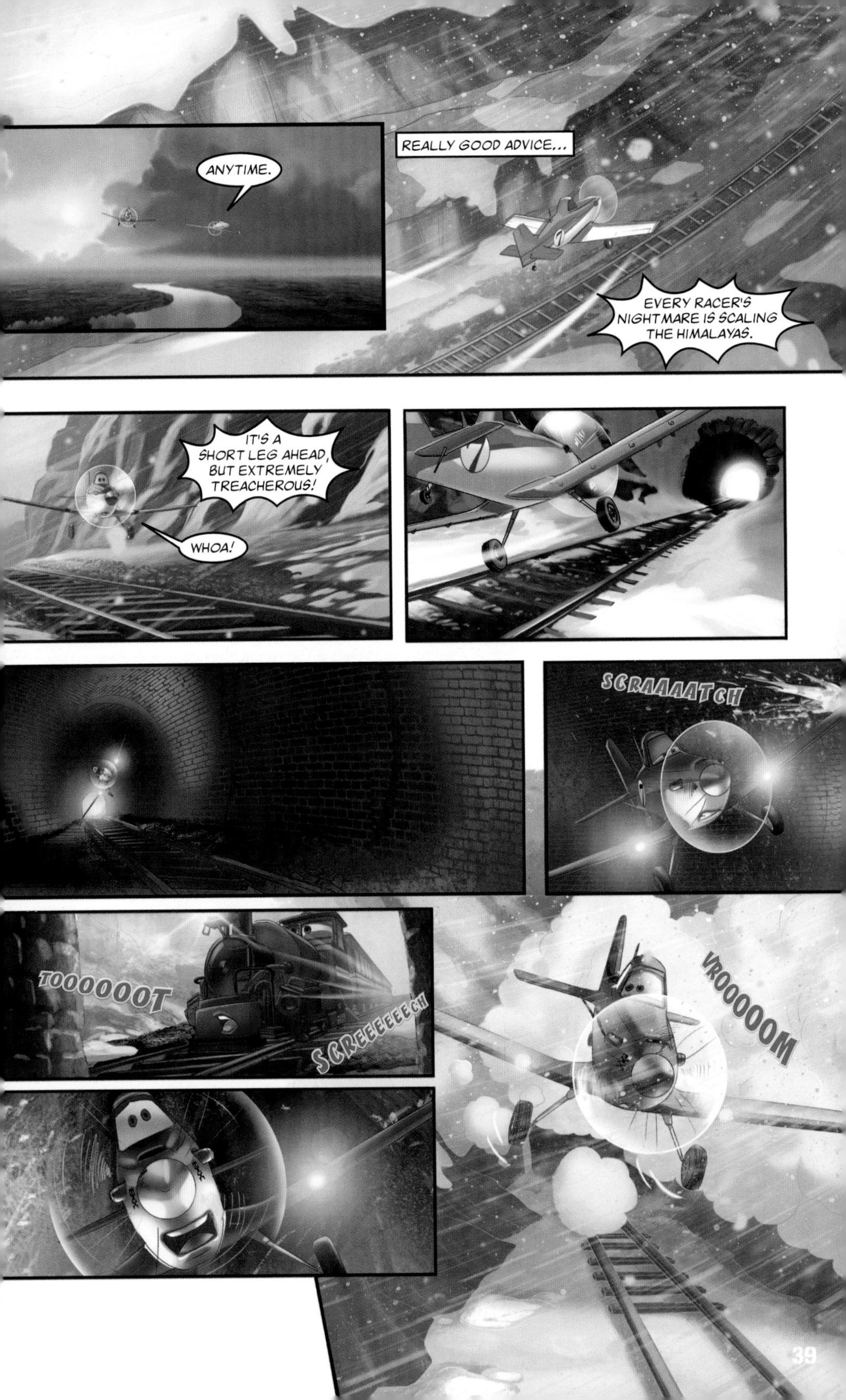
ANYTIME.
REALLY GOOD ADVICE...
EVERY RACER'S NIGHTMARE IS SCALING THE HIMALAYAS.
IT'S A SHORT LEG AHEAD, BUT EXTREMELY TREACHEROUS!
WHOA!
SCRAAAATCH
TOOOOOOT
SCREEEEEECH
VROOOOOM

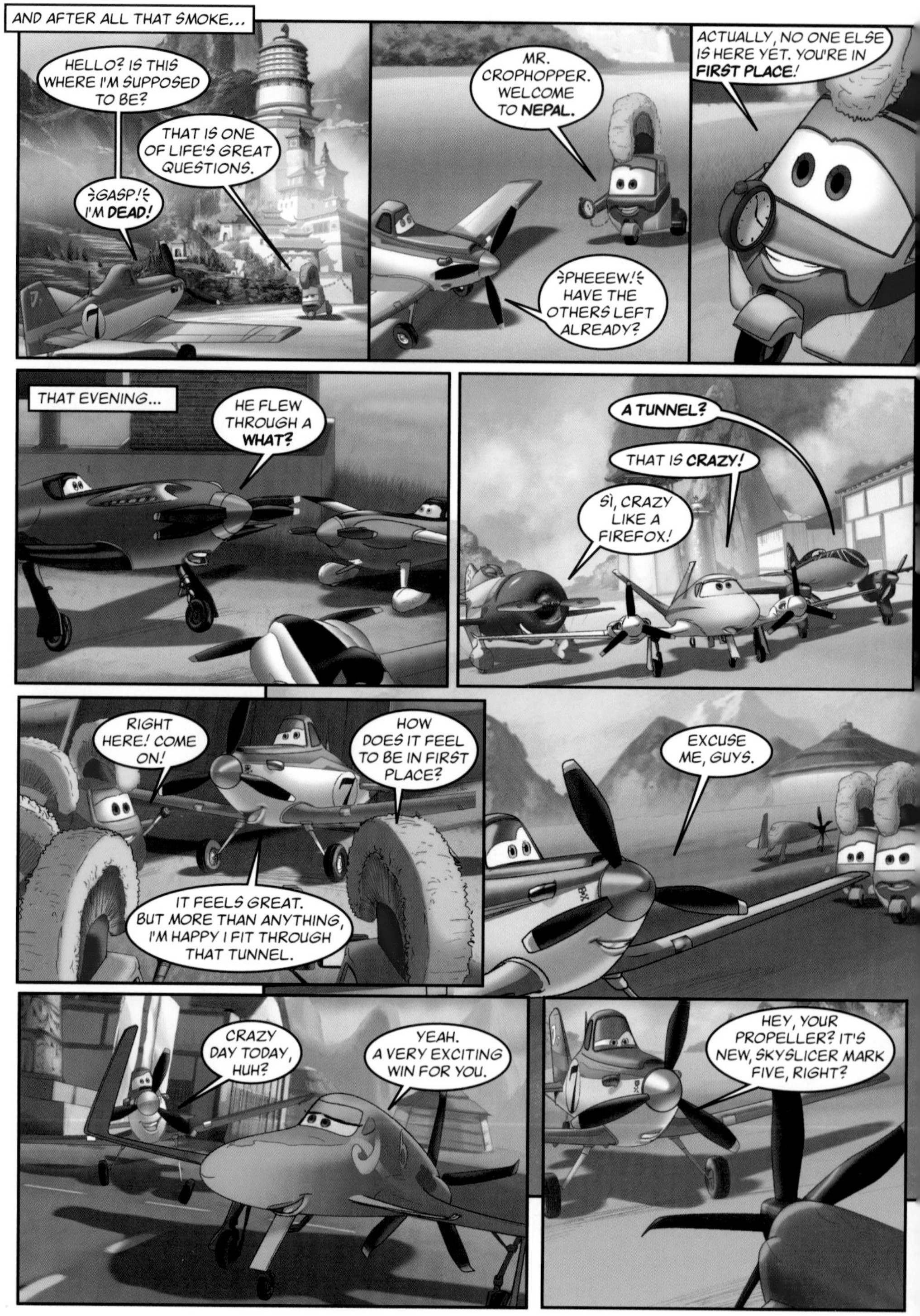

AND AFTER ALL THAT SMOKE...
HELLO? IS THIS WHERE I'M SUPPOSED TO BE?
THAT IS ONE OF LIFE'S GREAT QUESTIONS.
GASP! I'M DEAD!
MR. CROPHOPPER. WELCOME TO NEPAL.
PHEEEW! HAVE THE OTHERS LEFT ALREADY?
ACTUALLY, NO ONE ELSE IS HERE YET. YOU'RE IN FIRST PLACE!
THAT EVENING...
HE FLEW THROUGH A WHAT?
A TUNNEL?
THAT IS CRAZY!
SÌ, CRAZY LIKE A FIREFOX!
RIGHT HERE! COME ON!
HOW DOES IT FEEL TO BE IN FIRST PLACE?
IT FEELS GREAT. BUT MORE THAN ANYTHING, I'M HAPPY I FIT THROUGH THAT TUNNEL.
EXCUSE ME, GUYS.
CRAZY DAY TODAY, HUH?
YEAH. A VERY EXCITING WIN FOR YOU.
HEY, YOUR PROPELLER? IT'S NEW, SKYSLICER MARK FIVE, RIGHT?

...N'T THOSE MADE EXCLUSIVELY R **RIPSLINGER'S RACE TEAM?**

DUSTY, I...

I REALLY THOUGHT THAT YOU'D JUST TURN AROUND.

WELL, YOU WERE WRONG. AND I WAS WRONG ABOUT YOU.

OH, HEY, RIP. THANKS FOR FIRST PLACE.

...TRAL CHINA...

FLYING LOW AND QUICK, DUSTY CROPHOPPER IS MANAGING TO HOLD ON THE TOP SPOT.

BUT CURRENT REIGNING CHAMP RIPSLINGER IS JUST SECONDS BEHIND HIM!

...SHANGHAI'S PUDONG ...ERNATIONAL AIRPORT...

WE HEAD OUT ACROSS THE PACIFIC TOMORROW, SKIP.

YOU WERE STATIONED THERE FOR A WHILE. GOT ANY ADVICE?

BE CAREFUL.

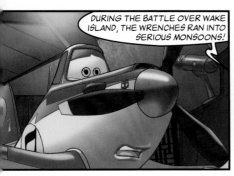

DURING THE BATTLE OVER WAKE ISLAND, THE WRENCHES RAN INTO SERIOUS MONSOONS!

AND ONE MORE THING...

... I'M **PROUD** OF YOU, DUSTY.

THANKS... "WINGMAN."

HEY, DUSTY, WE HAVE A SURPRISE FOR YOU!

WE'RE GONNA MEET YOU IN **MEXICO**! TICKETS ARE ON SPARKY AND ME!

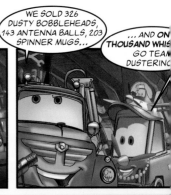

WE SOLD 326 DUSTY BOBBLEHEADS, 143 ANTENNA BALLS, 203 SPINNER MUGS...

... AND ON THOUSAND WHIS GO TEAM DUSTERING

LATER THAT NIGHT...

CLICK

...LOVE MACHINE!!!

NO! NO! NO! A THOUSAND NO'S!

SLAM

SOB!

QUE PASO? DUSTY, WHAT ARE YOU DOING?

CLICK

LOW AND SLOW.

TCHICA TCHIC

JUST A LOVE MACHINE...

AH, SEÑOR EL CHU... YOU'RE PRETTY ROMANTIC FOR A SHOW-OFF!

I AM IN YOUR DEBT, COMPADRE.

COMPADRE. I LIKE THAT.

...HE RACE CONTINUES!

NOT TOO BAD FOR A FARM BOY!

1. - DUSTY CROPHOPPER   9. - FA...
2. - RIPSLINGER   10. - TYS...
3. - NED   11. - SEC...
4. - ZED   12. - PIST...
5. - EL CHUPACABRA   13. - LITT...
6. - BULLDOG   14. - ROD...
7. - ISHANI   15. - FIRE...
8. - KANEDA

≶HUMPH.!≶

WHAT HAPPENED TO YOU?

THAT SONG... IT FLIPPED A SWITCH!

MY LITTLE MONSTER! COME HERE!

SHE IS LIKE A JAGUAR NOW!

LATER...

THIS IS OUR SIXTH AND LONGEST LEG. THESE RACERS WILL NEED TO FOLLOW THEIR GPS ANTENNAS...

...BECAUSE THERE'S A **BIG OCEAN** BETWEEN HERE AND MEXICO!

VROOAM

WHANGGG

WHOA!

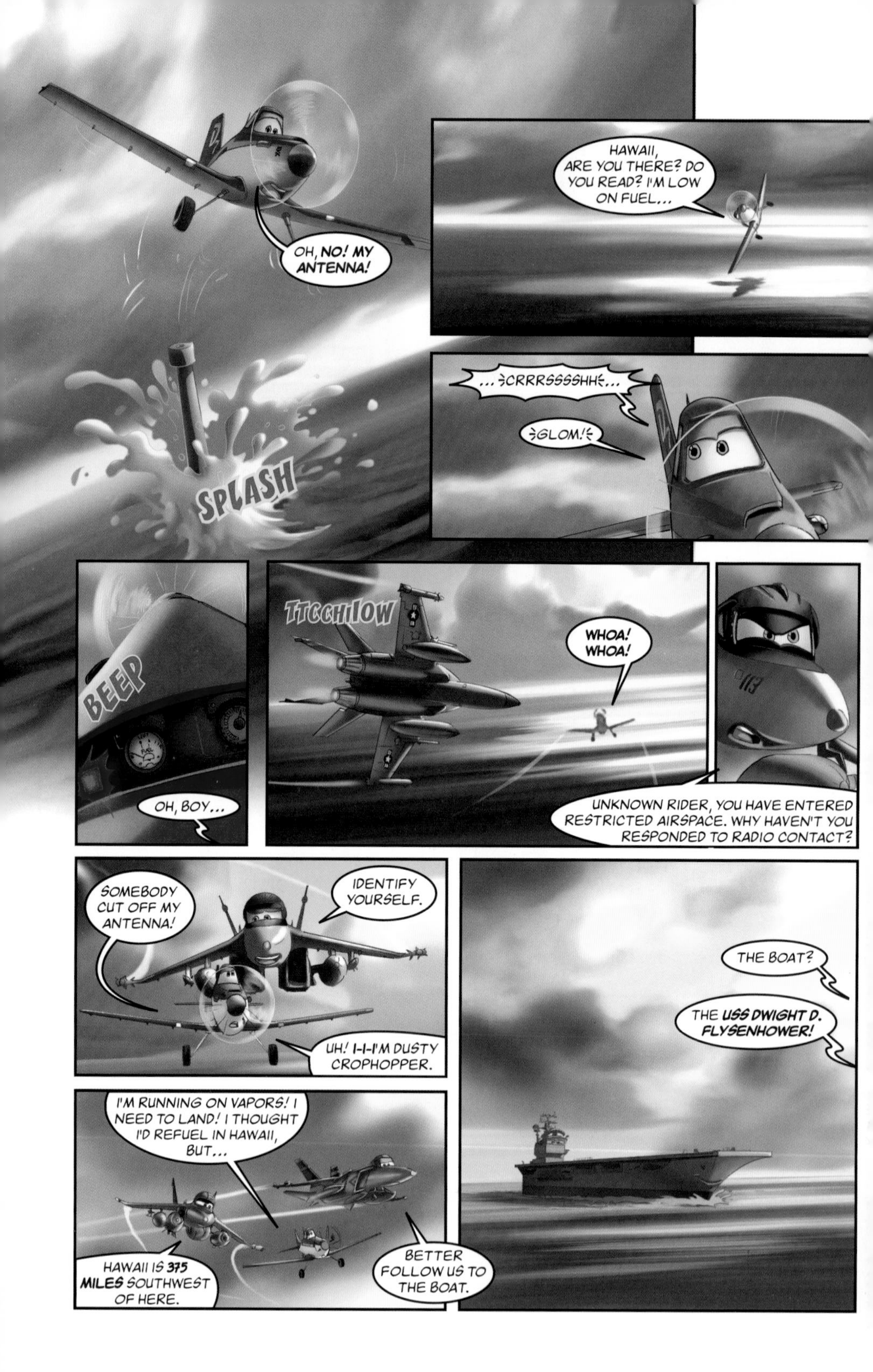
OH, NO! MY ANTENNA!
SPLASH
HAWAII, ARE YOU THERE? DO YOU READ? I'M LOW ON FUEL...
...CRRRSSSSHH...
GLOM!
BEEP
OH, BOY...
TTCCHILOW
WHOA! WHOA!
UNKNOWN RIDER, YOU HAVE ENTERED RESTRICTED AIRSPACE. WHY HAVEN'T YOU RESPONDED TO RADIO CONTACT?
SOMEBODY CUT OFF MY ANTENNA!
IDENTIFY YOURSELF.
UH! I-I-I'M DUSTY CROPHOPPER.
I'M RUNNING ON VAPORS! I NEED TO LAND! I THOUGHT I'D REFUEL IN HAWAII, BUT...
HAWAII IS 375 MILES SOUTHWEST OF HERE.
BETTER FOLLOW US TO THE BOAT.
THE BOAT?
THE USS DWIGHT D. FLYSENHOWER!

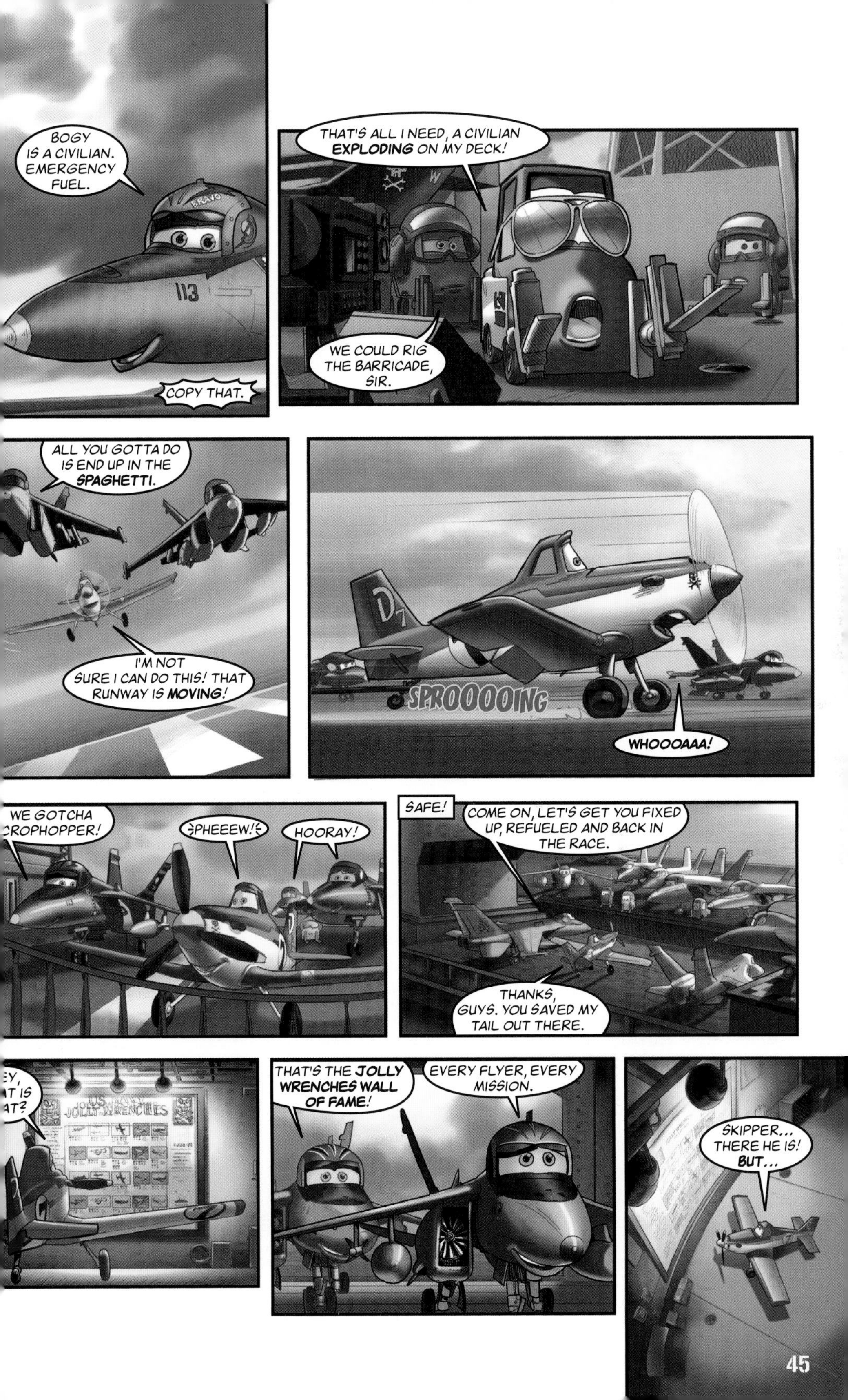
BOGY IS A CIVILIAN. EMERGENCY FUEL.
COPY THAT.
THAT'S ALL I NEED, A CIVILIAN **EXPLODING** ON MY DECK!
WE COULD RIG THE BARRICADE, SIR.
ALL YOU GOTTA DO IS END UP IN THE **SPAGHETTI**.
I'M NOT SURE I CAN DO THIS! THAT RUNWAY IS **MOVING**!
SPROOOOOING
WHOOOAAA!
WE GOTCHA CROPHOPPER!
PHEEEW!
HOORAY!
SAFE!
COME ON, LET'S GET YOU FIXED UP, REFUELED AND BACK IN THE RACE.
THANKS, GUYS. YOU SAVED MY TAIL OUT THERE.
THAT'S THE **JOLLY WRENCHES WALL OF FAME**!
EVERY FLYER, EVERY MISSION.
SKIPPER... THERE HE IS! **BUT...**

...WHY'S THERE ONLY **ONE** MISSION?

GLENDAL CANAL

MEANWHILE...

CHUG. WHAT'S ALL THAT?

I'VE NEVER BEEN OUT OF THE COUNTRY. GOTTA BE PREPARED, RIGHT?

SKIPPER?

COME IN, SKIPPER!

DUSTY? WE'RE HEADIN' OFF TO MEXICO RIGHT NOW!

GLAD YA GOT THERE SAFE. WEATHER REPORT SAYS A MAJOR STORM BREWIN' OUT THERE.

I'M NOT IN MEXICO. I'M WITH THE JOLLY WRENCHES.

YOU'RE ON TH FLYSENHOWE

I SAW THE WALL OF FAME... THEY ONLY LIST ONE MISSION FOR YOU.

IT MUST BE A MISTAKE...

LOOK YOU'VE GOTTA GET OUTTA THERE! YOU'RE GONNA HAVE TO **FLY HIGH**!

IS IT TRUE?

LISTEN TO M GET ABOVE T STORM...

SKIPPER! IS IT **TRUE**?

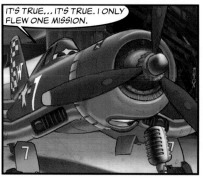

IT'S TRUE... IT'S TRUE. I ONLY FLEW ONE MISSION.

BUT ALL THOSE STORIES...

CROPHOPPER! WE'VE GOT WEATHER MOVING IN FAST.

46

ON DECK...

THE CAT WILL TAKE YA FROM ZERO TO 160 KNOTS IN **TWO SECONDS**.

YOU'VE GOT TO TAKE OFF! YOU DON'T GO NOW, YOU DON'T GO **AT ALL**.

ENGINE FULL THROTTLE, NOD TO THE SHOOTER WHEN YOU'RE SET.

GO WIN IT FOR THE WRENCHES, DUSTY! **VOLO PRO VERITAS!**

GO!

CLANK WOOOOSH

...ICO ...ATIONAL ...ORT...

SEÑOR RIPSLINGER, DO YOU HAVE ANY COMMENTS ON THE DISAPPEARANCE OF DUSTY CROPHOPPER?

DUSTY WAS A NICE GUY.

HE FLEW THE CHALLENGE AND PIERCED THE CLOUDS OF MEDIOCRITY. EXCUSE ME.

LET'S HOPE HE MAKES A BETTER BOAT THAN A PLANE.

THAT WAS A GOOD ONE, BOSS.

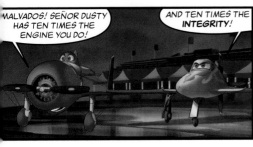

MALVADOS! SEÑOR DUSTY HAS TEN TIMES THE ENGINE YOU DO!

AND TEN TIMES THE **INTEGRITY!**

SAID THE PLANE WITH THE SHINY NEW PROPELLER,...

47

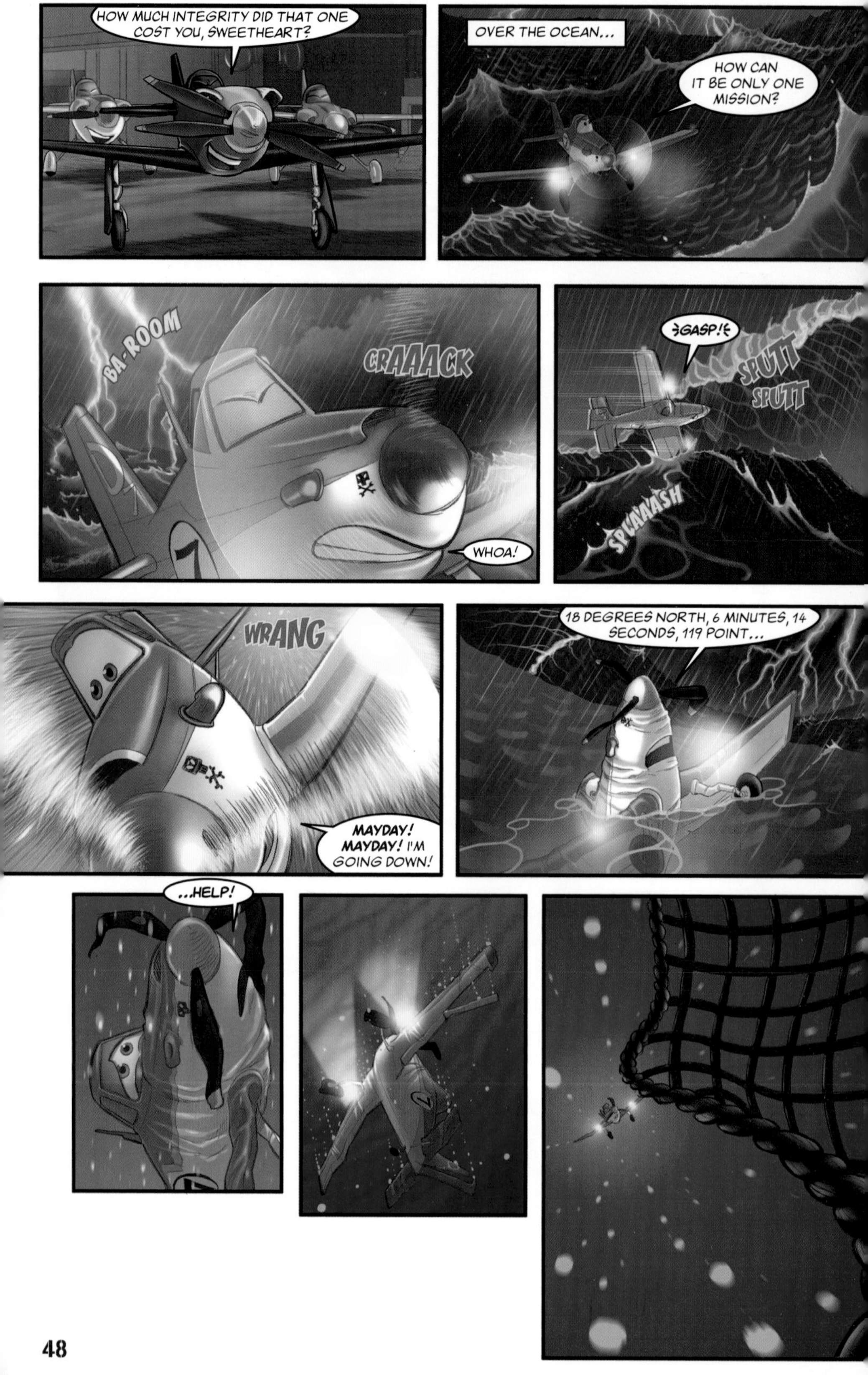
HOW MUCH INTEGRITY DID THAT ONE COST YOU, SWEETHEART?
OVER THE OCEAN...
HOW CAN IT BE ONLY ONE MISSION?
BA-ROOM
CRAAACK
WHOA!
GASP!
SPUTT
SPUTT
SPLAAASH
WRANG
MAYDAY! MAYDAY! I'M GOING DOWN!
18 DEGREES NORTH, 6 MINUTES, 14 SECONDS, 119 POINT...
...HELP!

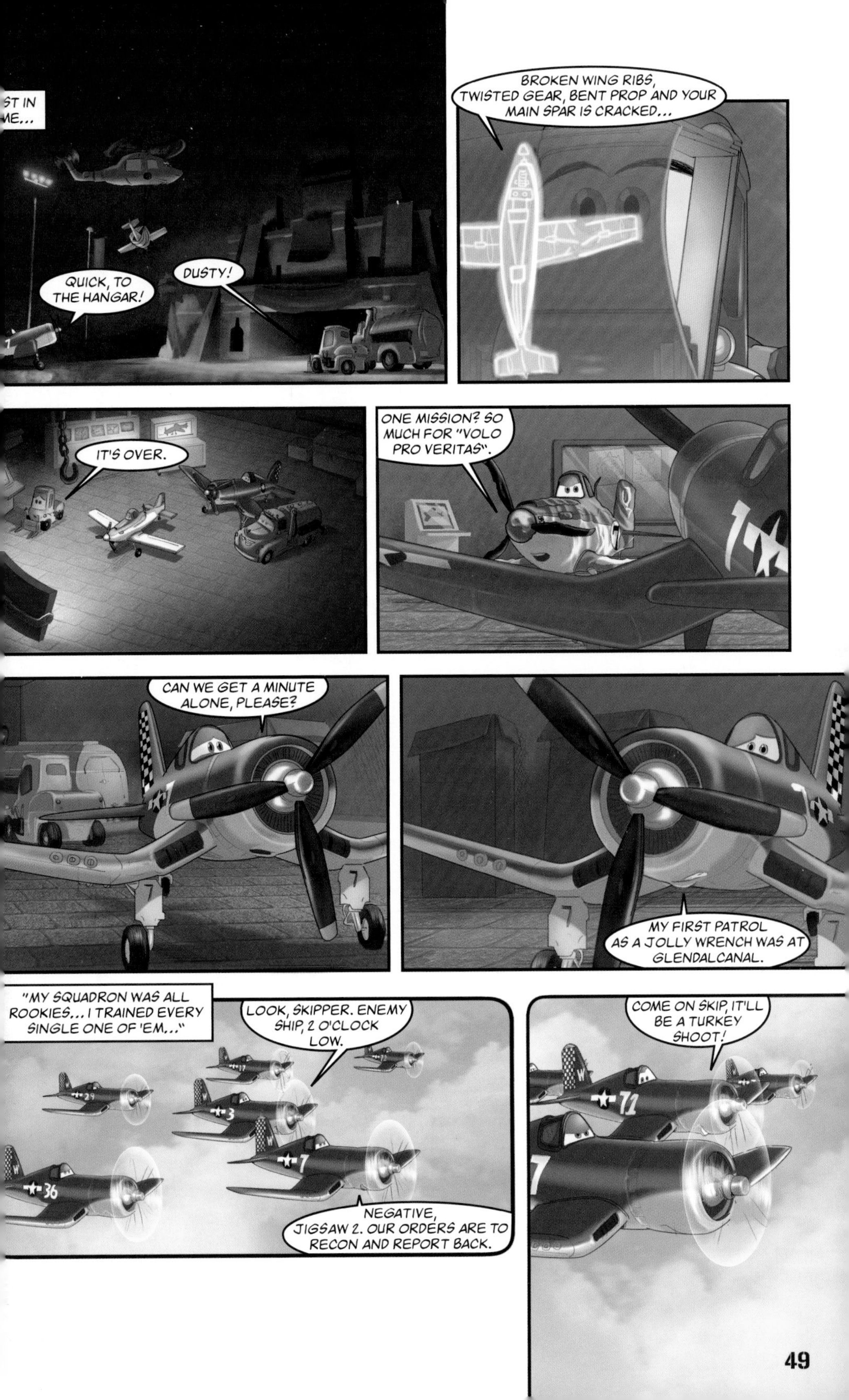

QUICK, TO THE HANGAR!
DUSTY!
BROKEN WING RIBS, TWISTED GEAR, BENT PROP AND YOUR MAIN SPAR IS CRACKED...
IT'S OVER.
ONE MISSION? SO MUCH FOR "VOLO PRO VERITAS".
CAN WE GET A MINUTE ALONE, PLEASE?
MY FIRST PATROL AS A JOLLY WRENCH WAS AT GLENDALCANAL.
"MY SQUADRON WAS ALL ROOKIES... I TRAINED EVERY SINGLE ONE OF 'EM..."
LOOK, SKIPPER. ENEMY SHIP, 2 O'CLOCK LOW.
NEGATIVE, JIGSAW 2. OUR ORDERS ARE TO RECON AND REPORT BACK.
COME ON SKIP, IT'LL BE A TURKEY SHOOT!

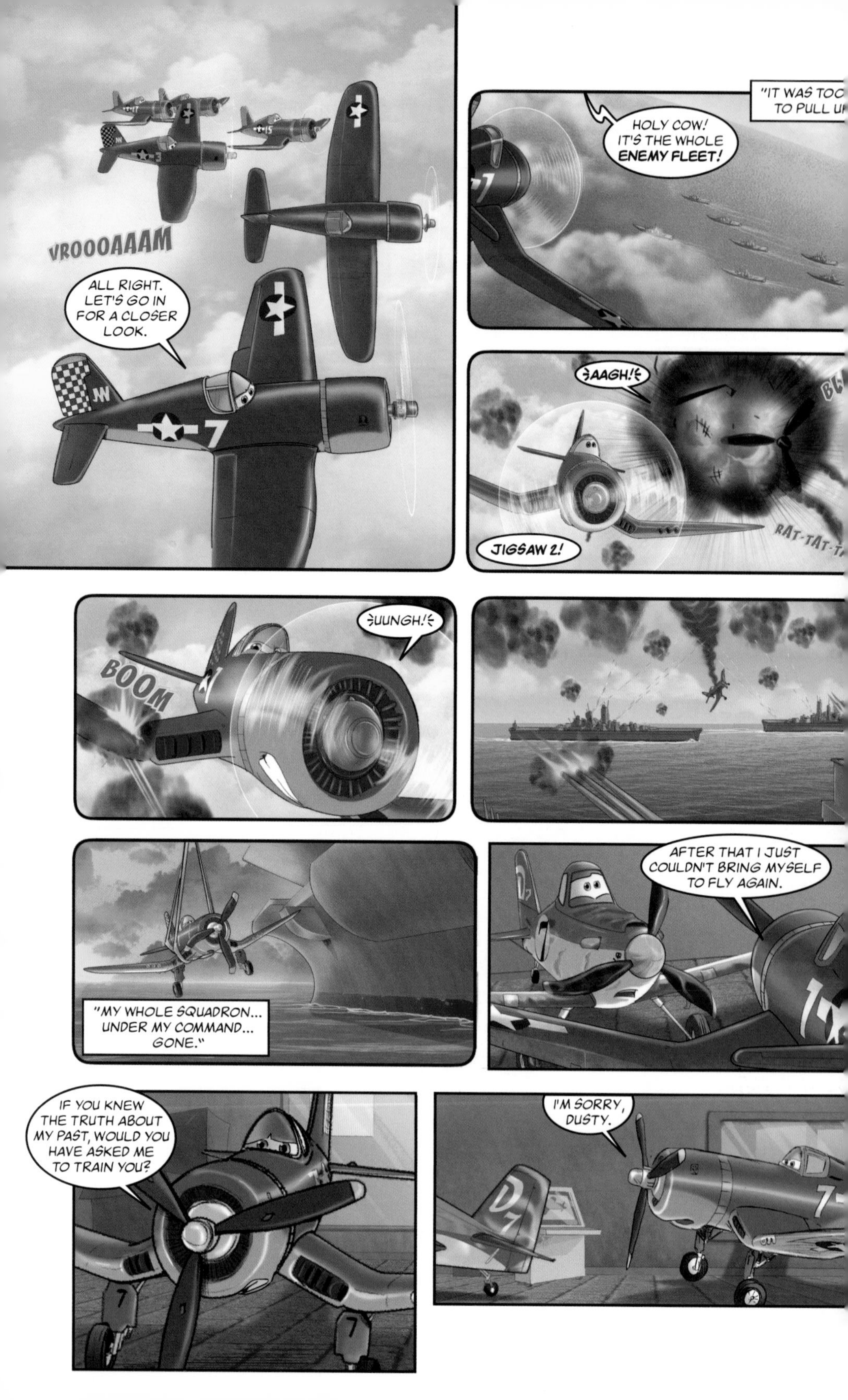

VROOOAAAM
ALL RIGHT. LET'S GO IN FOR A CLOSER LOOK.
"IT WAS TOO
TO PULL U
HOLY COW! IT'S THE WHOLE ENEMY FLEET!
AAGH!
JIGSAW 2!
RAT-TAT-T
UUNGH!
BOOM
"MY WHOLE SQUADRON... UNDER MY COMMAND... GONE."
AFTER THAT I JUST COULDN'T BRING MYSELF TO FLY AGAIN.
IF YOU KNEW THE TRUTH ABOUT MY PAST, WOULD YOU HAVE ASKED ME TO TRAIN YOU?
I'M SORRY, DUSTY.

DUSTY...?

CAN YOU BELIEVE IT? HE HASN'T BEEN STRAIGHT WITH ME THIS WHOLE TIME.

AT LEAST YOU WERE HONEST. YOU SAID I WASN'T BUILT FOR THIS.

IF YOU HAD LISTENED TO ME, I'D NEVER EVER FORGIVE MYSELF.

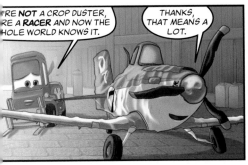

'RE **NOT** A CROP DUSTER, 'RE A **RACER** AND NOW THE HOLE WORLD KNOWS IT.

THANKS, THAT MEANS A LOT.

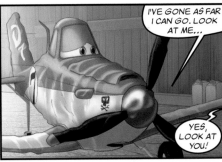

I'VE GONE AS FAR I CAN GO. LOOK AT ME...

YES, LOOK AT YOU!

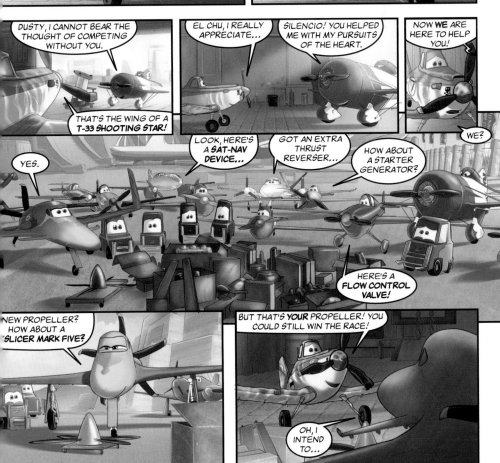

DUSTY, I CANNOT BEAR THE THOUGHT OF COMPETING WITHOUT YOU.

THAT'S THE WING OF A **T-33 SHOOTING STAR!**

EL CHU, I REALLY APPRECIATE...

SILENCIO! YOU HELPED ME WITH MY PURSUITS OF THE HEART.

NOW **WE** ARE HERE TO HELP YOU!

WE?

YES.

LOOK, HERE'S A **SAT-NAV DEVICE...**

GOT AN EXTRA THRUST REVERSER...

HOW ABOUT A STARTER GENERATOR?

HERE'S A **FLOW CONTROL VALVE!**

NEW PROPELLER? HOW ABOUT A 'SLICER MARK FIVE?

BUT THAT'S **YOUR** PROPELLER! YOU COULD STILL WIN THE RACE!

OH, I INTEND TO...

BUT WITH **MY OLD** PROPELLER. THIS ONE DIDN'T REALLY SUIT ME.

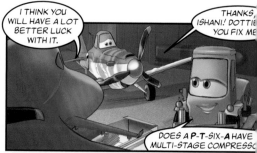

I THINK YOU WILL HAVE A LOT BETTER LUCK WITH IT.

THANKS, ISHANI! DOTTIE YOU FIX ME

DOES A **P-T-SIX-A** HAVE MULTI-STAGE COMPRESSO

"YES. **IT DOES!**"

THERE'S A LOT OF WORK TO

... BUT THERE'S ALSO TIME TO **STUDY THE OPPONENT!**

WHEN THE MORNING COMES,...

WHOA,... DUDE.

WE'LL SEE YOU IN NEW YORK!

HA! IT'S DUSTIN' TIME!

DUSTY!

HE'S BACK!

WHOA, WHO'S THAT GUY?

IT'S THE CROP DUSTER!

ANOTHER ONE?

IS THE SAME ONE, KNUCKLEHEAD!

BOLTING ON A FEW NEW PARTS DOESN'T CHANGE WHO YOU ARE.

YOU'RE AFRAID OF GETTING BEAT BY A CROP DUSTER.

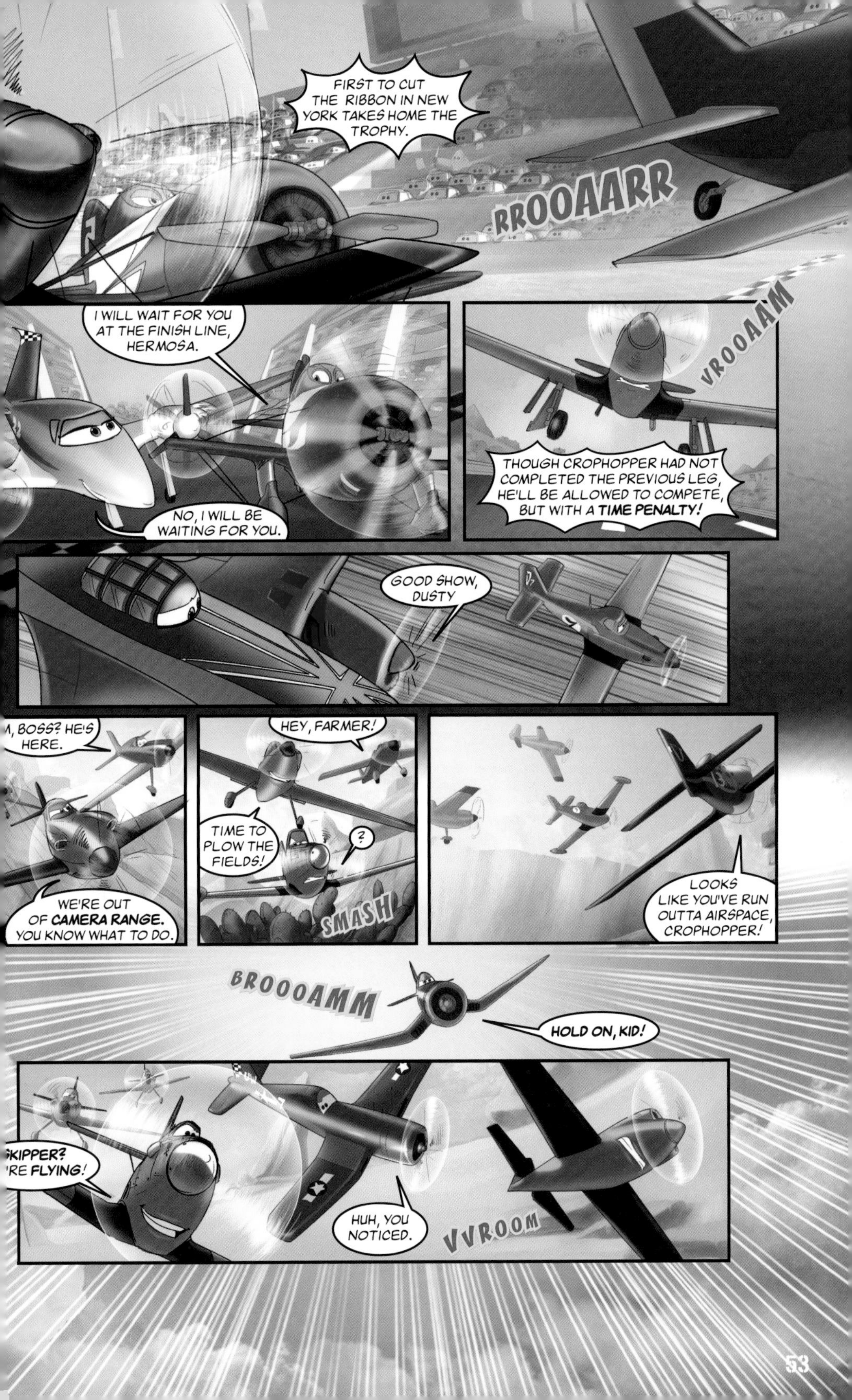

FIRST TO CUT THE RIBBON IN NEW YORK TAKES HOME THE TROPHY.
BROOAARR
I WILL WAIT FOR YOU AT THE FINISH LINE, HERMOSA.
NO, I WILL BE WAITING FOR YOU.
VROOAAM
THOUGH CROPHOPPER HAD NOT COMPLETED THE PREVIOUS LEG, HE'LL BE ALLOWED TO COMPETE, BUT WITH A **TIME PENALTY!**
GOOD SHOW, DUSTY
BOSS? HE'S HERE.
WE'RE OUT OF **CAMERA RANGE.** YOU KNOW WHAT TO DO.
HEY, FARMER!
TIME TO PLOW THE FIELDS!
?
SMASH
LOOKS LIKE YOU'VE RUN OUTTA AIRSPACE, CROPHOPPER!
BROOOAMM
HOLD ON, KID!
SKIPPER?
RE **FLYING!**
HUH, YOU NOTICED.
VVROOM

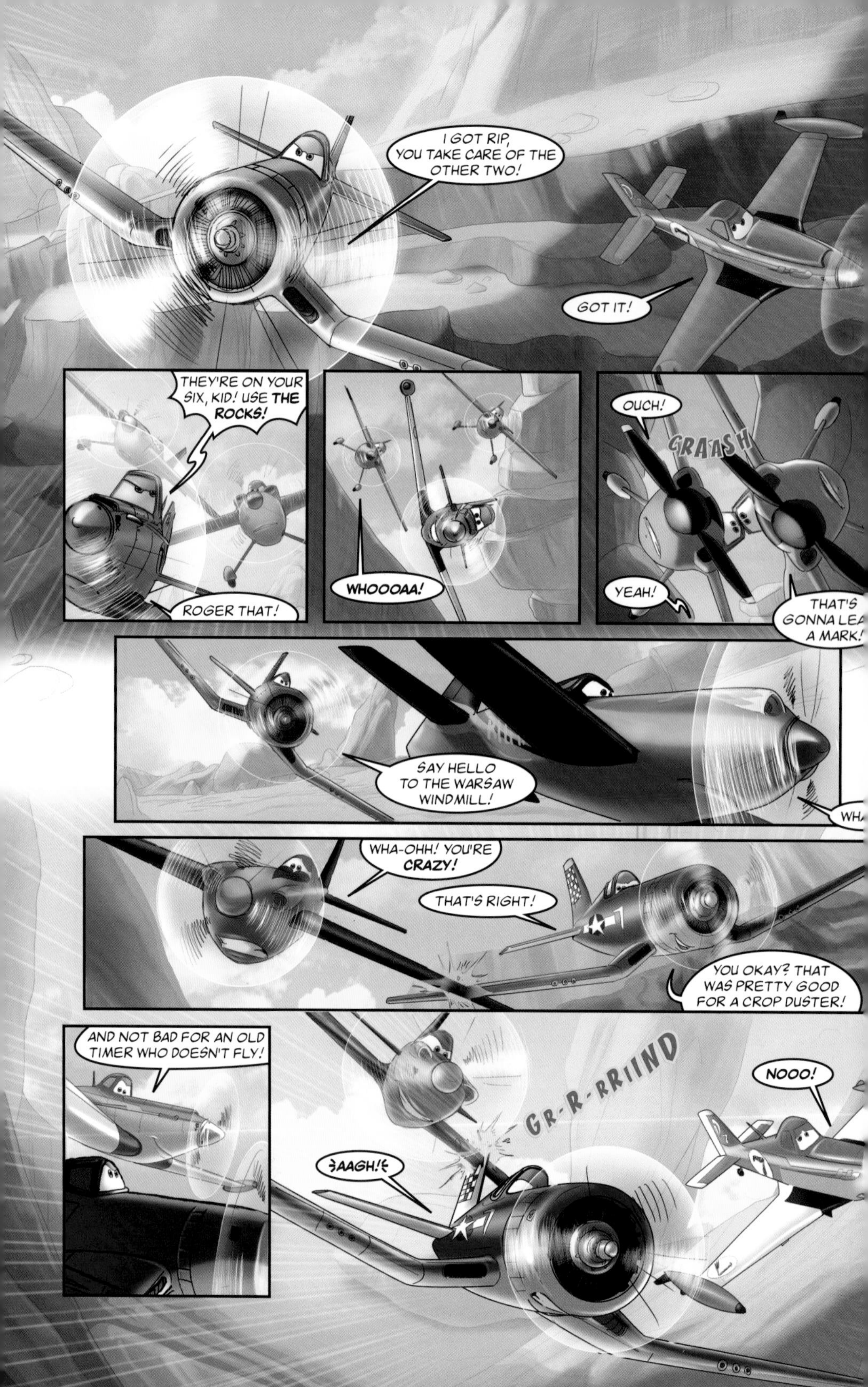
I GOT RIP, YOU TAKE CARE OF THE OTHER TWO!
GOT IT!
THEY'RE ON YOUR SIX, KID! USE **THE ROCKS!**
ROGER THAT!
WHOOOAA!
OUCH!
GRAASH
YEAH!
THAT'S GONNA LEA A MARK!
SAY HELLO TO THE WARSAW WINDMILL!
WHA
WHA-OHH! YOU'RE **CRAZY!**
THAT'S RIGHT!
YOU OKAY? THAT WAS PRETTY GOOD FOR A CROP DUSTER!
AND NOT BAD FOR AN OLD TIMER WHO DOESN'T FLY!
GR-R-RRIIND
NOOO!
AAGH!

THAT IS WHY THEY CALL 'EM SKYSLYCERS!

SKIPPER, ARE YOU OKAY?

YOU KIDDIN'? I'M GREAT!

GO GET HIM! GO!

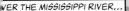...VER THE MISSISSIPPI RIVER...

WE'RE CLOSING IN ON THE FINAL STRETCH, FOLKS!

THAT'S RIGHT, COLIN, AND RIPSLINGER HAS MAINTAINED A FORMIDABLE LEAD!

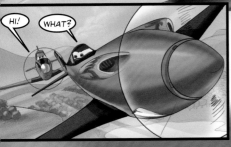

HI!

WHAT?

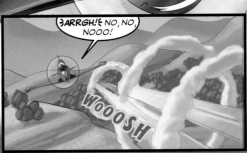

ⵣARRGH!ⵣ NO, NO, NOOO!

WOOOSH

"TAILWINDS LIKE NOTHING YOU'VE EVER FLOWN..."

ROGER THAT, SKIP!

DON'T LOOK DOWN! DON'T LOOK DOWN!

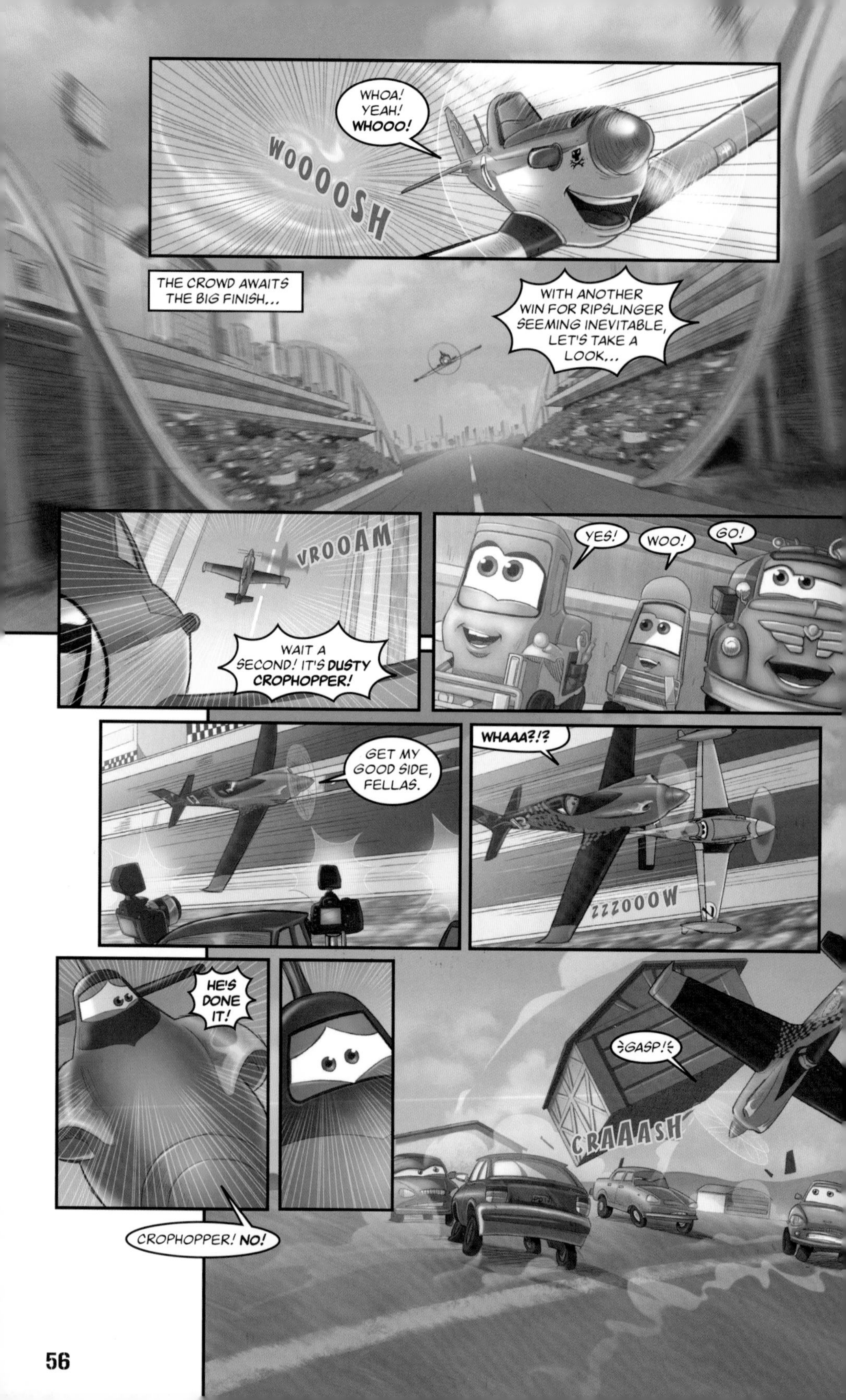
WHOA! YEAH! WHOOO!
WOOOOSH
THE CROWD AWAITS THE BIG FINISH...
WITH ANOTHER WIN FOR RIPSLINGER SEEMING INEVITABLE, LET'S TAKE A LOOK...
VROOAM
WAIT A SECOND! IT'S DUSTY CROPHOPPER!
YES!
WOO!
GO!
GET MY GOOD SIDE, FELLAS.
WHAAA?!?
WOOOZZZ
HE'S DONE IT!
CROPHOPPER! NO!
GASP!
CRAAASH

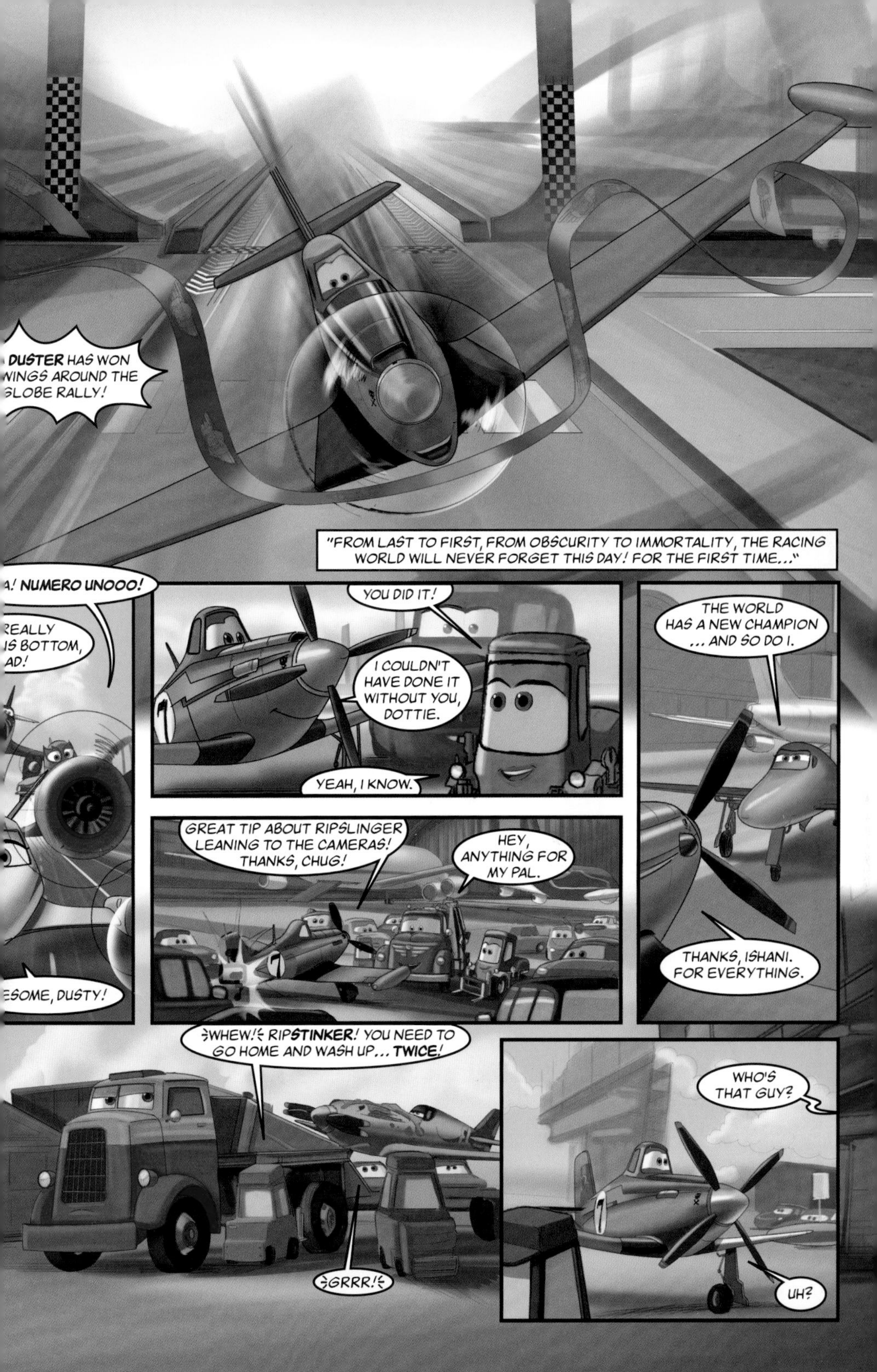
DUSTER HAS WON
WINGS AROUND THE
GLOBE RALLY!
"FROM LAST TO FIRST, FROM OBSCURITY TO IMMORTALITY, THE RACING WORLD WILL NEVER FORGET THIS DAY! FOR THE FIRST TIME..."
A! NUMERO UNOOO!
REALLY
IS BOTTOM,
AD!
ESOME, DUSTY!
YOU DID IT!
I COULDN'T HAVE DONE IT WITHOUT YOU, DOTTIE.
YEAH, I KNOW.
THE WORLD HAS A NEW CHAMPION ... AND SO DO I.
GREAT TIP ABOUT RIPSLINGER LEANING TO THE CAMERAS! THANKS, CHUG!
HEY, ANYTHING FOR MY PAL.
THANKS, ISHANI. FOR EVERYTHING.
WHEW! RIPSTINKER! YOU NEED TO GO HOME AND WASH UP... TWICE!
GRRR!
WHO'S THAT GUY?
UH?

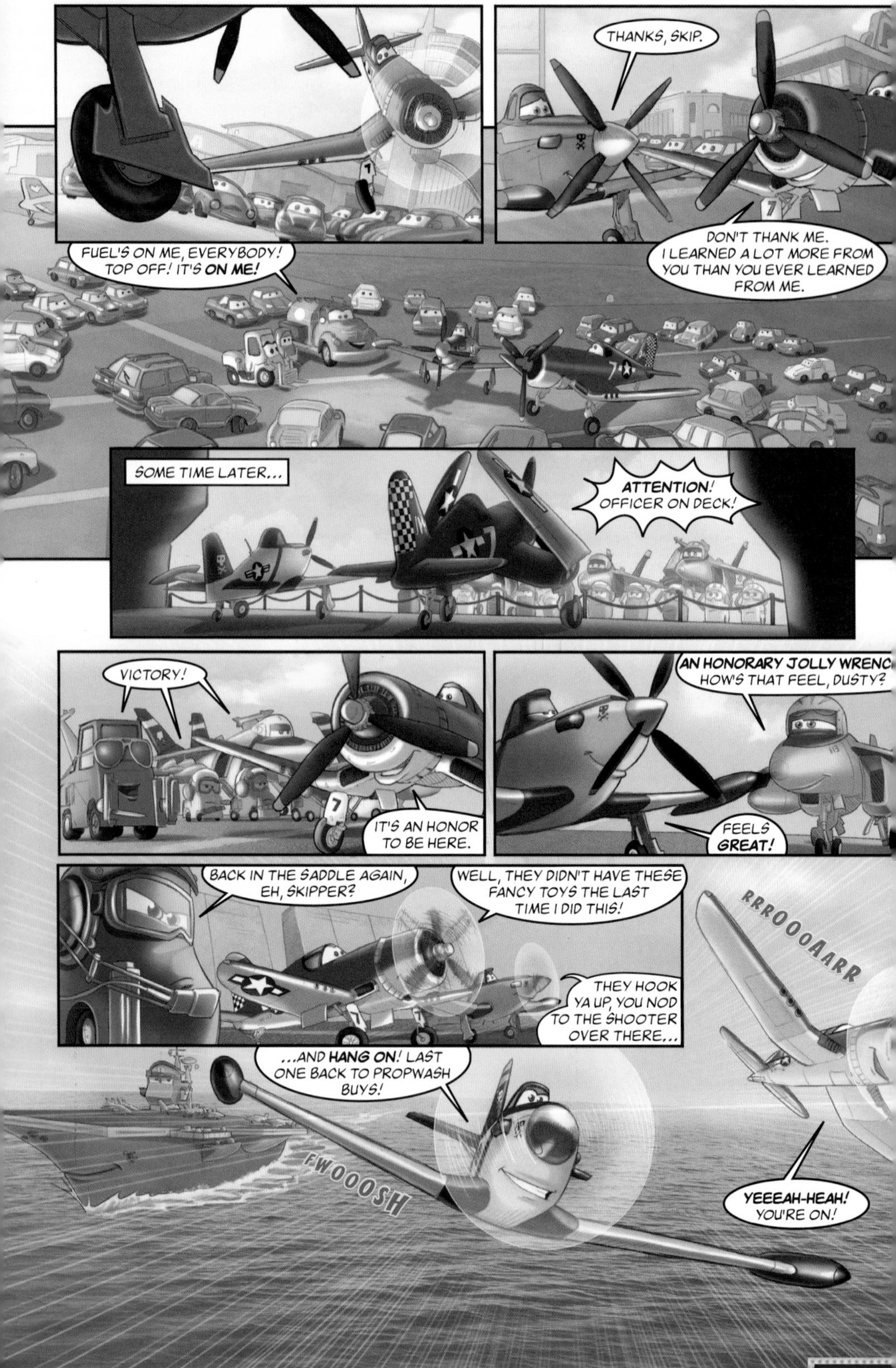
THANKS, SKIP.
FUEL'S ON ME, EVERYBODY! TOP OFF! IT'S ON ME!
DON'T THANK ME. I LEARNED A LOT MORE FROM YOU THAN YOU EVER LEARNED FROM ME.
SOME TIME LATER...
ATTENTION! OFFICER ON DECK!
VICTORY!
IT'S AN HONOR TO BE HERE.
AN HONORARY JOLLY WRENC
HOW'S THAT FEEL, DUSTY?
FEELS GREAT!
BACK IN THE SADDLE AGAIN, EH, SKIPPER?
WELL, THEY DIDN'T HAVE THESE FANCY TOYS THE LAST TIME I DID THIS!
THEY HOOK YA UP, YOU NOD TO THE SHOOTER OVER THERE...
RRROOOAARR
...AND HANG ON! LAST ONE BACK TO PROPWASH BUYS!
FWOOOSH
YEEEAH-HEAH! YOU'RE ON!
THE E

ATCH OUT FOR PAPERCUTZ

lcome to the high-flying premiere of
SNEY GRAPHIC NOVELS, a brand-new
ies from Papercutz, those crazy young
n and women in their flying machines,
licated to publishing graphic novels for all
s! Papercutz is also the very same publisher
o has been bringing you the adventures
Tinker Bell and all her fairy friends in the
SNEY FAIRIES graphic novel series for
past few years! I should know, I'm Jim
icrup, the Editor-in-Chief of Papercutz—
ich considering just these two titles is a
le like being an air traffic controller!

t unlike DISNEY FAIRIES, which features
nker Bell and all her fairy friends from
.ie Hollow in each and every graphic
vel, DISNEY GRAPHIC NOVELS will
featuring a rotating line-up of awesome
sney super-stars! Starring in our premiere
ume, is DISNEY PLANES, those amazing
aces we all know and love. But coming
ır way in the very next volume of DISNEY
APHIC NOVELS will be none other than
character who is virtually synonymous
h Disney—Mickey Mouse himself!
's starring in an all-new series where he
fronts and explores the supernatural in a
y that only he can! It's Mickey Mouse as
i've never seen him before battling ghosts
l goblins in a full-length graphic novel
enture! It's called X-MICKEY, and we're
e you're going to love it!

en coming up in the thrilling third volume
DISNEY GRAPHIC NOVELS will be
ollection of fun and fashionable stories
rring Minnie Mouse and Daisy Duck!

These two wonderful BFF are having all sorts of exciting times together and now you'll be able to frolic with them as well.

We're going to keep it a secret for now as to exactly what awaits you in DISNEY GRAPHIC NOVELS #4, but we will say it's nothing that you'll ever suspect! But we will tell you that in DISNEY GRAPHIC NOVELS #5, DISNEY PLANES returns with all-new stories starring Dusty Crophopper and his friends.

Way back in the very first DISNEY FAIRIES graphic novel I told you how thrilled I was to be working on Disney comics—that it was a dream come true. Now that we've added DISNEY GRAPHIC NOVELS I'm even more thrilled! When Papercutz publisher Terry Nantier and I first founded Papercutz, we could only dream about possibly publishing gaphic novels featuring comics from Disney. After all, we wanted to bring everyone the very best comics for all ages that we possibly could—and what could possibly be better than Disney?

Yet the most important thing is what you think! So please let us know—either write us a letter and mail it to the address below or send us an email! After all, we're doing all this for you. Let us know what you like and/or what you don't like. Then we'll do everything we possibly can to make DISNEY GRAPHIC NOVELS the very best comicbook experience possible for you!

Off we go!

Jim

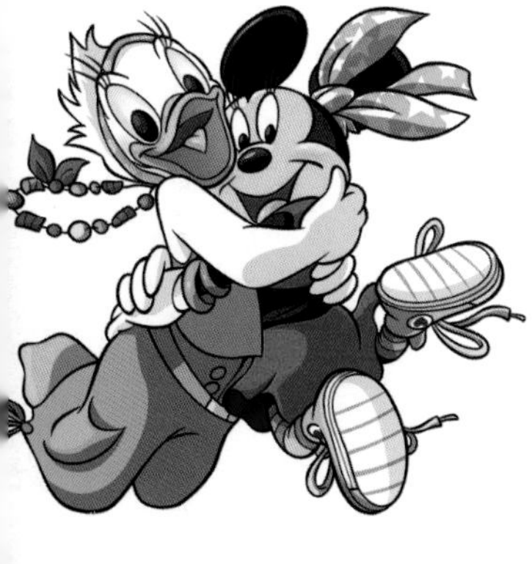

STAY IN TOUCH!

EMAIL: salicrup@papercutz.com
WEB: www.papercutz.com
TWITTER: @papercutzgn
FACEBOOK: PAPERCUTZGRAPHICNOVELS
REGULAR MAIL: Papercutz, 160 Broadway, Suite 700, East Wing, New York, NY 10038

Special Preview of DISNEY GRAPHIC NOVELS #2 "X-Mickey"...

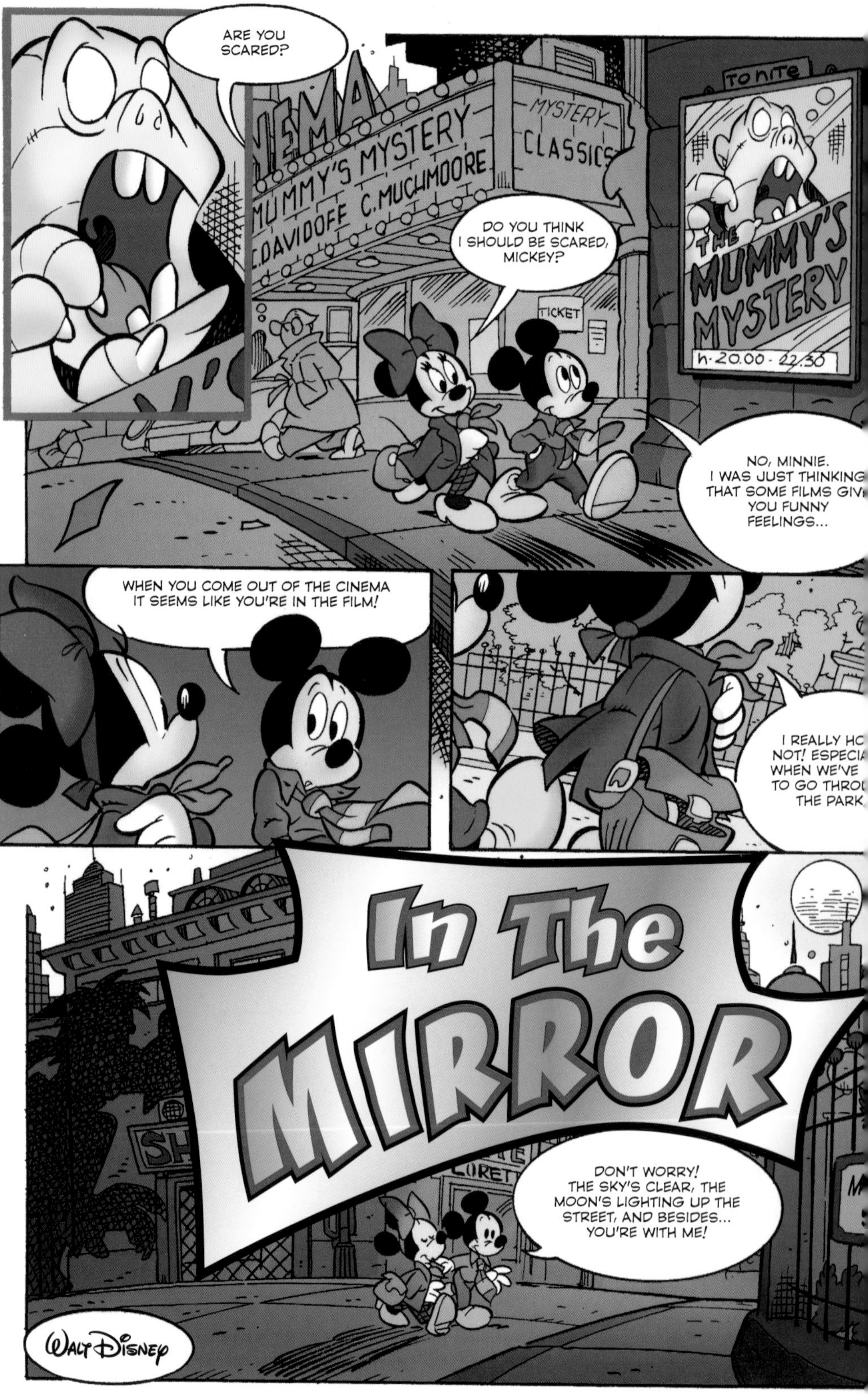
ARE YOU SCARED?
CINEMA
MUMMY'S MYSTERY
C.DAVIDOFF C.MUCHMOORE
MYSTERY CLASSICS
TONITE
THE MUMMY'S MYSTERY
h. 20.00 - 22.30
TICKET
DO YOU THINK I SHOULD BE SCARED, MICKEY?
NO, MINNIE. I WAS JUST THINKING THAT SOME FILMS GIV YOU FUNNY FEELINGS...
WHEN YOU COME OUT OF THE CINEMA IT SEEMS LIKE YOU'RE IN THE FILM!
I REALLY HC NOT! ESPECI WHEN WE'VE TO GO THRO THE PARK.
In The MIRROR
DON'T WORRY! THE SKY'S CLEAR, THE MOON'S LIGHTING UP THE STREET, AND BESIDES... YOU'RE WITH ME!
WALT DISNEY

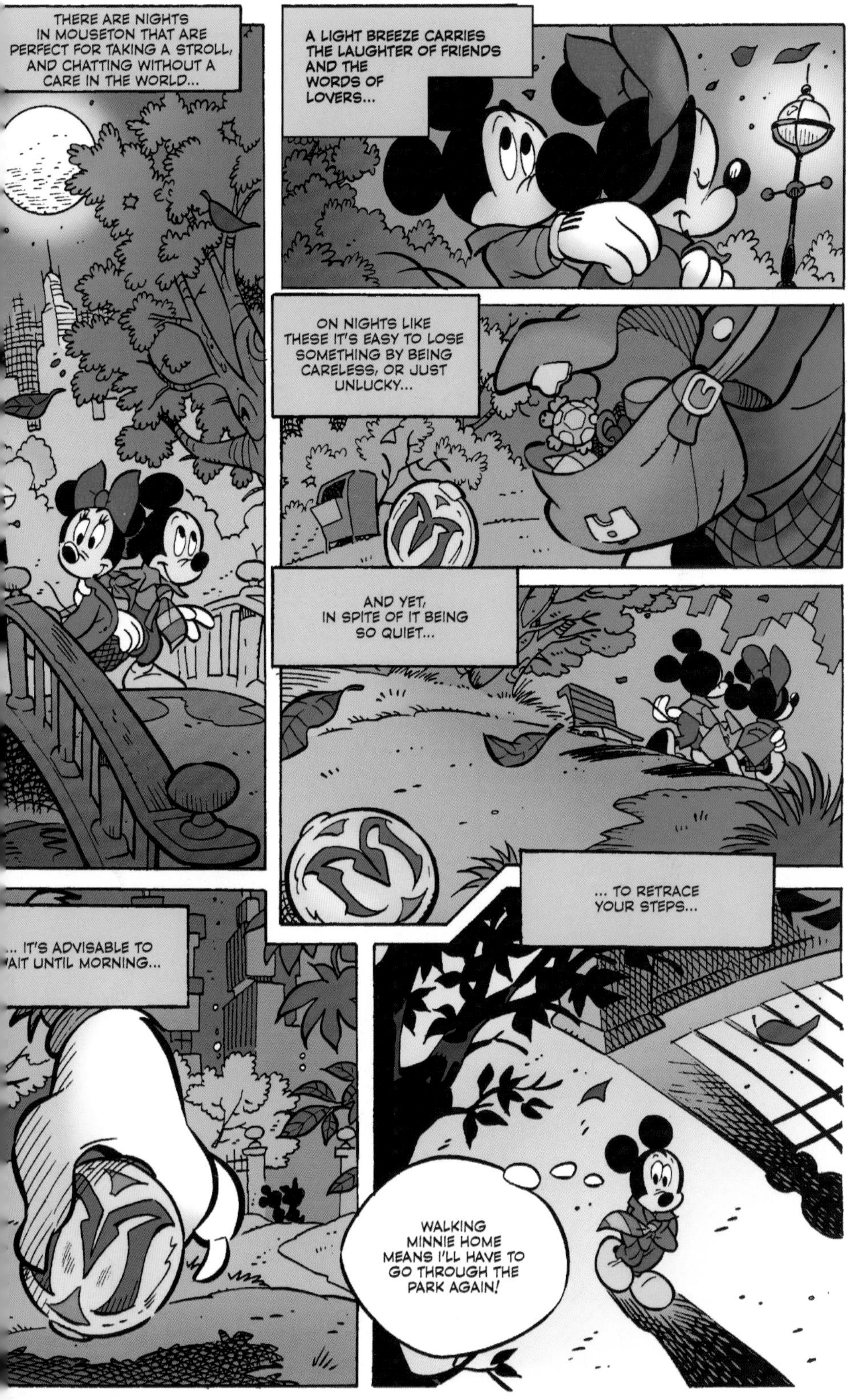
THERE ARE NIGHTS IN MOUSETON THAT ARE PERFECT FOR TAKING A STROLL, AND CHATTING WITHOUT A CARE IN THE WORLD...
A LIGHT BREEZE CARRIES THE LAUGHTER OF FRIENDS AND THE WORDS OF LOVERS...
ON NIGHTS LIKE THESE IT'S EASY TO LOSE SOMETHING BY BEING CARELESS, OR JUST UNLUCKY...
AND YET, IN SPITE OF IT BEING SO QUIET...
... IT'S ADVISABLE TO WAIT UNTIL MORNING...
... TO RETRACE YOUR STEPS...
WALKING MINNIE HOME MEANS I'LL HAVE TO GO THROUGH THE PARK AGAIN!

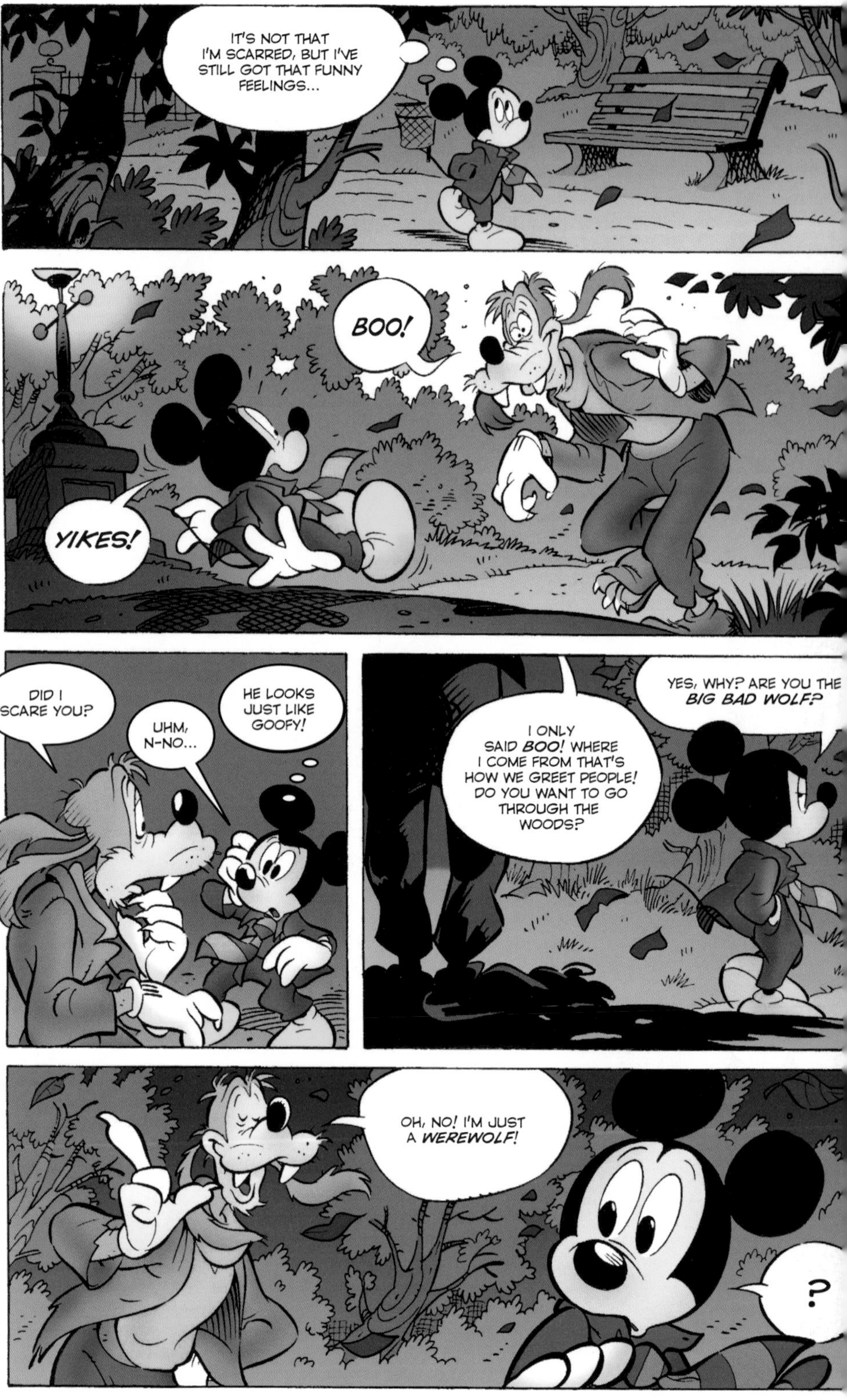
IT'S NOT THAT I'M SCARRED, BUT I'VE STILL GOT THAT FUNNY FEELINGS...
BOO!
YIKES!
DID I SCARE YOU?
UHM, N-NO...
HE LOOKS JUST LIKE GOOFY!
YES, WHY? ARE YOU THE BIG BAD WOLF?
I ONLY SAID BOO! WHERE I COME FROM THAT'S HOW WE GREET PEOPLE! DO YOU WANT TO GO THROUGH THE WOODS?
OH, NO! I'M JUST A WEREWOLF!
?

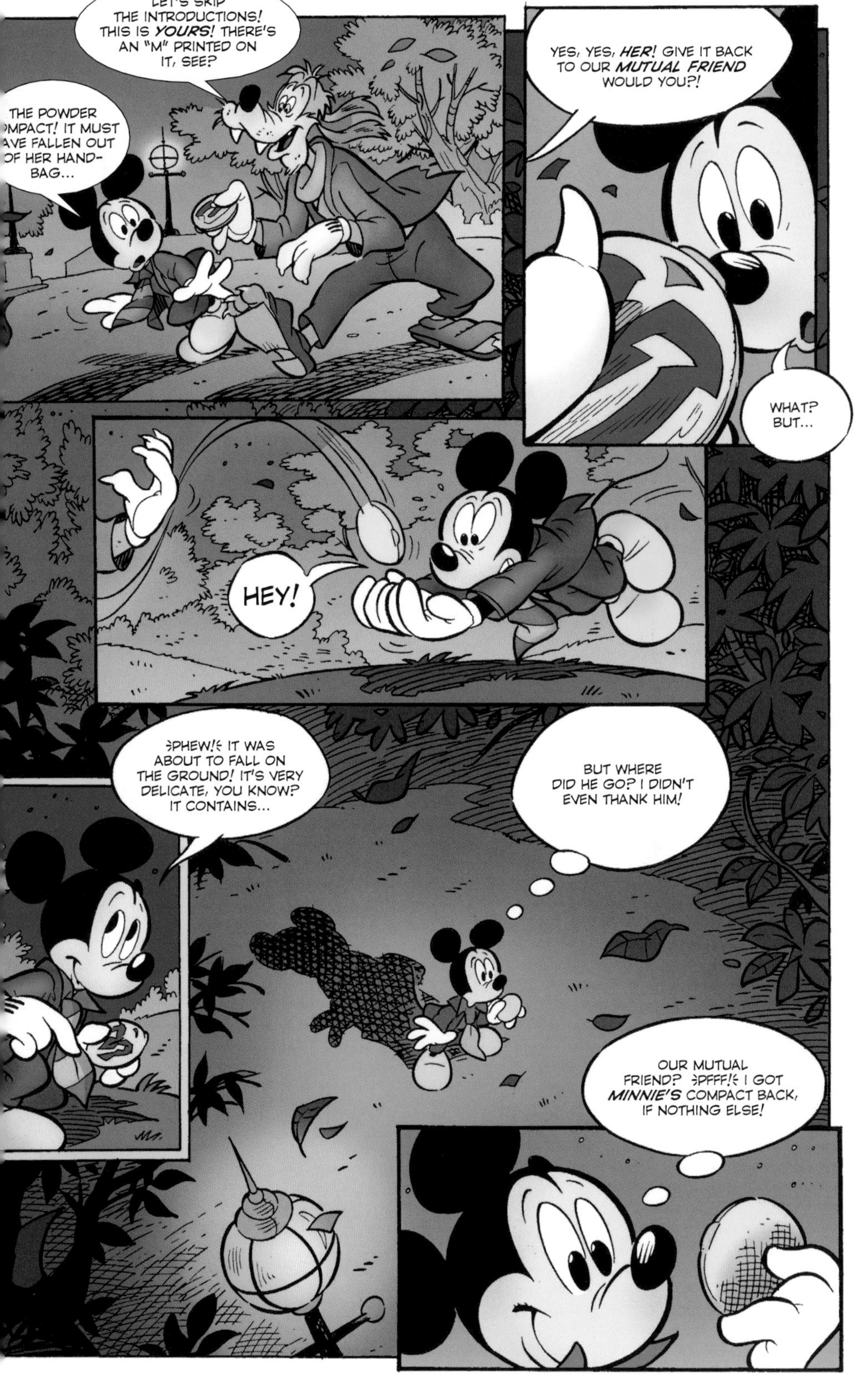
LET'S SKIP THE INTRODUCTIONS! THIS IS *YOURS!* THERE'S AN "M" PRINTED ON IT, SEE?
THE POWDER MPACT! IT MUST AVE FALLEN OUT OF HER HAND-BAG...
YES, YES, *HER!* GIVE IT BACK TO OUR *MUTUAL FRIEND* WOULD YOU?!
WHAT? BUT...
HEY!
PHEW! IT WAS ABOUT TO FALL ON THE GROUND! IT'S VERY DELICATE, YOU KNOW? IT CONTAINS...
BUT WHERE DID HE GO? I DIDN'T EVEN THANK HIM!
OUR MUTUAL FRIEND? PFFF! I GOT *MINNIE'S* COMPACT BACK, IF NOTHING ELSE!

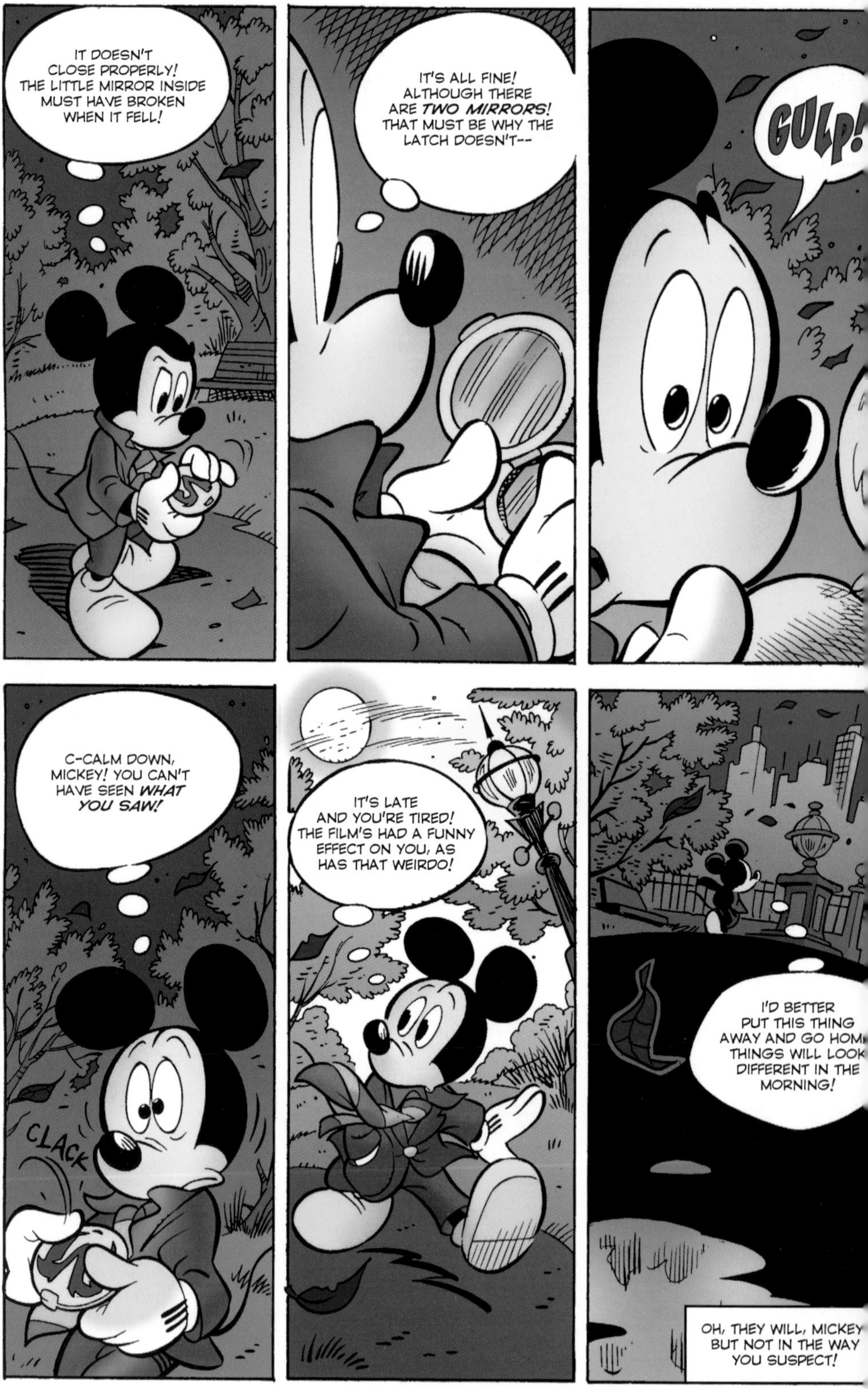
IT DOESN'T CLOSE PROPERLY! THE LITTLE MIRROR INSIDE MUST HAVE BROKEN WHEN IT FELL!
IT'S ALL FINE! ALTHOUGH THERE ARE *TWO MIRRORS!* THAT MUST BE WHY THE LATCH DOESN'T--
GULP!
C-CALM DOWN, MICKEY! YOU CAN'T HAVE SEEN *WHAT YOU SAW!*
CLACK
IT'S LATE AND YOU'RE TIRED! THE FILM'S HAD A FUNNY EFFECT ON YOU, AS HAS THAT WEIRDO!
I'D BETTER PUT THIS THING AWAY AND GO HOM THINGS WILL LOOK DIFFERENT IN THE MORNING!
OH, THEY WILL, MICKEY BUT NOT IN THE WAY YOU SUSPECT!

Don't miss DISNEY GRAPHIC NOVELS #2 "X-Mickey"—Coming Soon!